MAKE UP YOUR MIND THIS VERY MINUTE

This is going to be your greatest holiday season ever! You are going to have a sensational time this year throughout the entire festive holiday period. No hassles, no headaches, no depression, and most important, no holiday blues. This is not only going to be your first stress-free-end-of-the-year celebration, it is going to surpass your wildest expectations about what a holiday season can be. You are about to embark on—in a word—your very first *no-limit* holiday.

ALSO BY DR. WAYNE W. DYER

Real Magic
Your Erroneous Zones
Pulling Your Own Strings*

*coming soon

Available from HarperPaperbacks

NO MORE HOLIDAY BLUES

(formerly *Happy Holidays!*)

- UPLIFTING ADVICE FOR RECAPTURING
THE TRUE SPIRIT OF CHRISTMAS,
HANUKKAH, AND THE NEW YEAR

Dr. Wayne W. Dyer

HarperPaperbacks
A Division of HarperCollinsPublishers

HarperPaperbacks   *A Division of* HarperCollins*Publishers*
                   10 East 53rd Street, New York, N.Y. 10022

A hardcover edition of this book was published under the
title *Happy Holidays!* by William Morrow & Company,
Inc. in 1986. It is reprinted here by arrangement with
Arthur Pine Associates, Inc. Portions of this book appeared
in *Family Circle*.

A trade paperback edition of this book
was published in 1990 by HarperPerennial.

Cover photograph by Marybeth

First HarperPaperbacks printing: December 1993

Printed in the United States of America

HarperPaperbacks and colophon are trademarks of
HarperCollins*Publishers*

10 9 8 7 6 5 4 3 2 1

For my brother David:
That delightful child inside of you
always makes the holiday season
a glorious time of year for all of us.

■ CONTENTS

No More
Holiday Blues

Introduction

I love the holiday season more than any other time of the year. It is a very special feeling when I know that we are closing in on Christmas and Hanukkah. I have many wonderful memories of being a child at this time of the year, and that child inside of me is still very much alive and kicking today. One particular incident seems to stand above all of the others. I always did my own shopping as a young boy, even though it was often completed with very little money. I can remember going to the dime store and spending hours looking for a present for my mother. Ultimately

I ended up with a glass powder holder with a small deer on the top. The total cost was eighty-five cents, yet it was something that I felt so proud of as a small boy. I took home the deer powder container and wrapped it up without the benefit of a box, and then placed it under the Christmas tree and for days teased my mother to guess what I had bought her for Christmas. She would hold it in her hand and turn it over several times always saying, "I just can't guess, but I'm not going to open it until Christmas morning." Inside I couldn't wait for the big day to arrive for everyone to see what I had picked out to give. I always wanted them to open their presents early, because the wait seemed endless for me. Today, some thirty-five years later, my mother still has her precious memories of that glass deer powder holder that I bought as a ten-year-old boy.

The message of this book is all wrapped up in that little anecdote above. If you can get back to that time of your life when you were a child, enjoying every aspect of this glorious season, you can rid yourself of the "holiday blues" permanently. As a child, the shopping was something that filled you with excitement, and you were able to ignore the crowds. The time you spent decorating, wrapping, celebrating, worshiping, and being with your family was a pure delight. You still have that child inside of you, and you can let him/her escape at this time of the year and rekindle that flame of ecstasy rather than choosing to be gloomy over the holiday season. During this special time of year I regularly urge myself to let the children's laughter remind me how I used to be. This is a central theme of this little book. Remember how you used to be, each and every moment of this holiday season, and try hard to provide everyone with the seeds for future memories of a glorious holiday.

Each of the four chapters of this book offers a very special message to you at this time of the year, and is designed to be of specific help in making this the best season for you and those you love. My objective in writing them was to provide useful ideas that can be implemented every day. If you decide to follow some of the suggestions offered throughout the pages of this book, I am confident that you will find yourself having the time of your life, rather than drearily awaiting the end of the holidays.

The first chapter sets the stage for making this the best holiday season ever. It is written with the idea of rekindling the childhood flame that burns in each one of us, even though you may have let it become dimmer over the years. If you take on some childlike attitudes this holiday season, and use some of the specific strategies offered in this chapter, you will see yourself embracing the holidays rather than being a victim of them.

In Chapter 2 I have detailed many specific ideas for turning this time of the year into a no-limit experience for you and all of your loved ones. It focuses on helping you to shift around self-defeating attitudes and to look for the joy and ecstasy that is inherent in all celebrations, regardless of your ethnic or religious background. You can make the decision to have a no-limit holiday, and I have provided many suggestions to help you do just that.

The third chapter will aid you in taking advantage of each and every present moment that you have throughout the entire holiday time period. It examines the folly of making New Year's resolutions, since all of us live our lives in present moments rather than present years. The *now* is quite simply the working unit of your life, and learning how to live in it totally, will help you not only during the holiday season, but through each and every now of your life.

The final chapter deals with how to avoid the holiday letdown, and to turn what often becomes a negative experience into something to love and enjoy. The holiday-season letdown must be viewed as a choice, and consequently it is something that you can also choose to disavow. It is a self-defeating choice that many people make at this time of year, and I guarantee you that if you follow the suggestions in this chapter you will shift this holiday season from an experience of pique to a peak experience, without even having to make a big effort.

Today I view the holidays through the eyes of my five children. I watch how they jump with excitement every time they see Santa or Hanukkah candles or fes-

tive lights in the neighborhoods. I glow inside and out
as they talk about what to get Mommy or Grandma. I
stop to take in the fantastic smells of cookies baking. I
love to see their faces as they stop thinking about their
own little problems and totally tune in to this time of
the year. They love everything about it. They can't
seem to get enough of it. That is the joy for me—to see
others basking in the beautiful messages of this holiday
season. Whatever your circumstances in life, wherever
you live, regardless of how things used to be, this is it.
. . . This is your only holiday season to celebrate. If you
stop for a moment to think about what you can do to
make this particular season the best one you've ever
had, you will find the way to make it happen. That's
what this book is all about. Indeed, as you look around
you this year, look with new eyes at how to make it all
work for you, and while you are at it, "let the children's joy and laughter remind you how you used to
be."

ONE

The Holidays Are for Children
So Be a Child Again!

Remember how excited you used to be about the approaching holiday season? How you would get all knotted up inside with enthusiasm and hardly be able to contain your anticipation? Remember how you thought that it would absolutely never arrive, and how thrilled you were to participate in all of the events that made up the holidays for you? In case you've forgotten, the holiday season was once the most delightful time of the year for you. And the reason that it was so delicious and fun had to do with your being a child and consequently looking at the

DR. WAYNE W. DYER

world through childlike eyes. You didn't judge the seasonal activities, you simply enjoyed them. You can recapture that childlike approach to the holidays, as well as to the rest of life, if you will voluntarily shed some of the "grown-up" attitudes and beliefs that you've adopted since you left that wonderful world of childhood behind you.

As adults, we have come to believe that the holiday season is really only for children. You hear it all the time . . . "If it weren't for the children we wouldn't even celebrate," or "I just love to see the excitement of the children. Except for them I wouldn't even enjoy it because of the crowds, expense, and bother of it all." Thus only children can enjoy the holidays: Adults must suffer through them. For you to begin to enjoy the upcoming holiday season, you are going to have to forget this idea and remind yourself that "the season to be jolly" is not the exclusive domain of any one group, and that you have just as much of a right to make this the most joyous time of the year NOW, as you did when you had those visions of sugar plums dancing in your head so many years ago.

How did it happen? How did the most beautiful season of all get turned around into one that is full of hardship and even despair for so many? The real answer is that many of us have forgotten how to be childlike. The focus has somehow shifted from appreciation and excitement to work and travail. You can adopt new attitudes, reflecting the way you once viewed the

12   •

holiday season as opposed to the way you may look at it today. This little chart will illustrate some of those contrasting attitudes and expectations.

These contrasting attitudes point out how a child views the holidays from a positive perspective—up, excited, and full of awe—and how that very same child turns into an adult who eventually twists it around and ends up viewing the entire process as a negative, costly, and down experience. The truth is that the child who loved everything about the holiday period is still residing within you. You can in fact change your attitudes and make this time of the year the most perfect for yourself and your family by recapturing that child and letting him/her rule you during the next few weeks.

You may have come to believe that because you pay all of the bills, assume the responsibilities, do the chores, and generally work extra hard during the holiday period, it is impossible for you to have that innocent, childlike appreciation for this time of the year. This is patently false and something that you must challenge. You and only you must take responsibility for your own fulfillment, whether it be Christmas, Hanukkah, or an Independence Day picnic. If you have become overburdened during the holiday season, then it is because you have willingly adopted this role for yourself. Certainly you can teach others how to assume some of the responsibilities and change those things about the season that make it tiring and diffi-

CHILDLIKE VERSUS NEUROTIC ADULT ATTITUDES
TOWARD THE HOLIDAY SEASON

CHILDLIKE ATTITUDES	NEUROTIC ADULT ATTITUDES
"I can't wait to see all of the lights and decorations every place. Aren't they pretty?"	"They put those decorations up earlier every year. I can't believe they are doing it already."
"It sure is fun to see the stores full of people and all of the special gifts displayed."	"Christmas is becoming more commercial every year. I hate the crowds and the pushing and shoving."
"I don't think the big day will ever get here. . . . I just can't wait."	"I don't think this season will ever end. It seems to get longer every year."
"Let's send out holiday cards to everyone we know."	"Let's send out fewer cards this year by eliminating those who didn't send us cards last year."

CHILDLIKE VERSUS NEUROTIC ADULT ATTITUDES
TOWARD THE HOLIDAY SEASON *(Continued)*

CHILDLIKE ATTITUDES	NEUROTIC ADULT ATTITUDES
"What can I buy for Grandma, Billy, my teacher, the neighbors . . . ?"	"I don't think I should do anything for those people. They aren't that important to me."
"Boy oh boy, we get to see everyone in the family, that's what I love about the holidays."	"We have to put up with those neverending, boring relative gatherings again."
"We get to have a big dinner with all the trimmings."	"We have to go to all the trouble of fixing dinner, and for what?"
"I love to see all of the toys, decorations, trees . . ."	"This gets more expensive every year. I'll probably go into debt until next July."
"I really love all of my presents, thank you so much, everybody."	"I got another bunch of useless gifts that I'll only have to exchange. More lines to stand in."

CHILDLIKE VERSUS NEUROTIC ADULT ATTITUDES
TOWARD THE HOLIDAY SEASON *(Continued)*

CHILDLIKE ATTITUDES	NEUROTIC ADULT ATTITUDES
"I can't believe it's over already, it seems like it just started."	"Thank God it's over. If it lasted one more day I'd have had a nervous breakdown."

cult for you. But the first thing that you can do is shift around your attitudes and beliefs.

Just because you have overspent your budgeted allowance during the Christmas shopping season is no reason to become depressed. Obviously depression is not going to put additional funds into your bank account. Moreover, being annoyed by the crowds, or dismayed at the behavior of your relatives, or mad at a sales clerk, is not going to make those things change to suit you. Your thoughts and emotions about everything are under your own control! You can decide exactly how you are going to view all aspects of this holiday season. Anytime you choose reactions that make you unhappy or immobilized you are participating in the neurotic practice of adopting self-defeating rather than self-enhancing reactions to your world.

In terms of the childlike versus neurotic-adult attitudes mentioned in the chart on pages 14–16, you can decide to change your expectations this holiday season by adamantly taking the following stances on items in that list.

- Resolve to use the pretty decorations as reminders of how beautiful this time of the year really can be. Every time you see colored lights on a house or a particularly beautiful display, stop for a moment and reflect on the beauty of what you see. Don't use the presence of the decorations to remind yourself about anything negative. Refuse to allow those self-deprecating thoughts into your head, and say to anyone within earshot of you, "I love to see people dressing up the neighborhood and lighting up the world with beautiful lights and displays." In other words, see the decorations as reminders of the beauty of the season, as a child might, rather than as a reminder of all the things you have to do before the holidays arrive, as an adult would.

- Slow yourself down when shopping for holiday gifts. Make the experience of shopping and being out in the world something that you enjoy for itself, rather than as a necessary barrier that you must overcome on your way to having a nice holiday. Try to keep in mind how much you loved doing your holiday shopping as a child, then stop to say something kind to a harried sales clerk, sit and watch the people, ask questions about the new toys and electronic gadgets on the market, give some money to the charity collector, slow down and enjoy the scents of Christmas trees and wreaths, just as you did as a child. Give yourself permission to enjoy *all* aspects of this holiday season. When you take away the pace and go out into the world to shop and enjoy everything that you are going to encounter in the day, you'll have a set of expectations, even as you leave the house, that will permit you to enjoy everything that you are going to do in the day. A day of shopping is going to be dreadful, only if YOU set out anticipating it to be that way.

• Stop viewing the holiday period as one long season, and instead vow to enjoy every little facet of it for yourself. For example, make gift wrapping a total experience in itself, rather than a chore that you must accomplish before some self-imposed deadline. In addition, vow to appreciate rather than depreciate all activities, including shopping, card writing with the children, decorating with everyone involved, and meal preparation. Be spontaneous in each of these activities as well as creatively original. Make each thing you do fun and an experience unto itself, instead of one big headache that has many unbearable component parts. That's precisely how children approach everything in the Christmas season. Cookie making, stocking stuffing, caroling, wrapping presents, decorating, and so on, are all in-dividual fun things to the children, and can be for you as well.

- Vow to yourself that you are going to find some-thing to enjoy in every gift you receive, and that you are going to point out what you appreciate about the gift to the individual who took the time to think of you with a present. Forget about what the gift does for you, and remember that the real beauty of this particular gift is in the thoughtfulness of one other human being toward you. Force your-self to take an extra moment to say something nice to the giver, and stop selfishly thinking about how to return it, or why you don't like it, or having some other self-defeating reaction.

In order to become more childlike you should not think of yourself as having to give up being an adult. It is not necessary to become infantile and irrespon-sible in order to be a child again. The fully inte-grated person is capable of being both an adult and a child simultaneously. This means being able to be silly, to go along with a gag, to laugh and make jokes, to be nutty and know how to enjoy playing. It means giving up some of the masks of adulthood, and substituting fun and enjoyment. Being a child means wide-eyed excitement, spontaneous appreci-ation, cutting loose, and being full of awe and won-der at this magnificent universe.

The next time you walk by a schoolyard, watch the children playing. Notice how they are involved totally in what they are doing, how they scrap and run everywhere they go. Notice how they are oblivious to future problems that are just as real to them as yours are to you. They have to go to class in the afternoon, they have tests to take, friends who concern them, teachers who annoy them, and many many more difficulties to confront in their young lives. But somehow they have that magic quality of being able to suspend their troubles and simply let loose. It is almost as if they have given themselves permission to be free and they show it by becoming totally absorbed in their play.

Perhaps you believe that becoming more child-like is easier to say than do. You may be defending your position with sentences like, "Sure, I'd love to be a child and have nothing to worry about, but I've got a family to feed, responsibilities to consider, financial worries, and many other problems. How can I be a child and be a responsible adult as well?" When you argue for your problems, the only thing you get are your problems. I am not suggesting that one must be irresponsible to become more of a child. You can have both. But you can become a person who enjoys his or her tasks rather than is defeated by them. You can attack all of the responsibilities you have with a little less seriousness, and you can make all of your goals more fun to accomplish. Or you can maintain your position of having to be an adult and having to be solemn forever. Your problems will still be the same; the only difference will be that you won't enjoy yourself as much. Being childlike has nothing to do with responsibilities. Rather, it concentrates on developing an attitude of wide-eyed enthusiasm about everything that you undertake or observe.

The obsessive adult gives up his ability to be compulsive and fun-loving in the name of being grown up and dignified. The holidays are a good time to discard some of those overly "adult" behaviors and try to become more of a child again. Who knows, maybe your childlike but responsible behaviors will become permanent, year-round facets of the new you. I guarantee you that you'll be a happier person for it. For example, try:

- *Laughing!* Young children love to laugh; in fact, all of us love to be around people who have a sense of humor. The more laughter we have in our lives, the better everything seems to be. Children love teasing and being teased in a good-natured way. They go out of their way to linger a bit longer with someone who will make them laugh, and who can go along with a joke. We all seek out the quality of humor and laughter, and it is the one absolutely sure-fire way to eradicate depression. You simply cannot be depressed, anxious, nervous, or even sick and enjoy laughing at the same time. During the holidays try to become more of a child by permitting yourself to laugh more readily. Take an afternoon off to go to a movie, to the circus, or do something that will be a happy, humorous experience. Treat the holiday crowds lightly, have fun with the children, and see if this kind of attitude won't in fact make you have a glorious season, as well as a happier life all year long.

- *Fantasizing!* Children love to dream, to make up stories, to use their imagination, and so would you if you let yourself. Have you ever noticed how children will play a game called House, School, Bank, Hospital, or anything else that strikes their fancy? They become absorbed in the fantasy. They dress the part, they take on the role of given bank officials, their imaginations work for hours. Children also love to draw, to write poetry, to hear stories, to make up their own games, and to wander aimlessly into their mental excursions with anyone who is willing to listen or participate. Take them up on it! The Christmas and Hanukkah holiday season is one filled with rich fantasies for children. All of the Santa Claus stories, the lighting of candles, the presents, the reindeer, angels, and partridges in pear trees are what make this such a bountiful time of the year.

Fantasy is not only great fun, it is very healthy as well. If you allow yourself the luxury of fantasizing and dreaming sometimes, you'll soon find that many of those very things that were only fantasies will ultimately become realities. If you never give yourself permission to dream about something in the future, you'll never have an opportunity to realize anything different than what you have. The more you allow yourself to be dreamy-eyed and to fantasize, the more you'll create an opportunity to change your life for the better.

• *Allow yourself to have that "crazy" quality.* Children are silly, they act dumb and "crazy" a great deal, and for them, it is a terrific way to be. But you may have sent that crazy quality out of your life in favor of being more mature and sensible. The idea of being a bit zany and unpredictable may sound foolish to you, but the child in you really enjoys being that way sometimes. A holiday party, for example, is a perfect setting for adults to become a bit silly: to wear funny clothes, to loosen up a bit, to not worry about what others may think of you. These kinds of party-going behaviors need not be restricted to special occasions, nor must they be associated with booze or drugs. The more often you permit yourself to be childishly crazy, the more fun you are going to have in your life.

Being crazy is all tied up with letting go of some of the controls that restrict your life. You can certainly be serious on the job, be mature about how you face your responsibilities, and earnest in attacking problems that call for a straightforward, no-nonsense approach. But the ability to loosen up will aid you not only in having more fun, but will help you be even more effective when it is time for seriousness. The ability to "regress" at will, to act kooky and silly, is in fact a very admirable trait. Some people find it exceedingly difficult to ever let go and be a bit wild. They are afraid of what they might do, or they are intimidated by being less than dignified and shedding the ceremonial garb that is in fact their assumed personality. If you observe people whom others enjoy being around, you'll find out they often possess that unpredictable quality of being a bit crazy.

This holiday season is the perfect time for you to become a little zany. Give some funny gifts, dress up as Santa, and enjoy yourself instead of being predictable and stodgy. Play some silly games on Christmas morning, or perhaps throw a neighborhood party and invite people to whom you've hardly spoken all year. Give up the mask of seriousness and see how good it feels. If you do it now, during the holiday season, you'll find it easier to do the rest of the year as well.

- *Be more spontaneous.* Notice how children are willing to try anything without even having a plan. The child inside of you wants to be spontaneous and adventuresome, without having to think things through in advance. You want to just go out and do new things, and have that same excitement about new things that you had when you were much younger. All children have this spark of spontaneity inside of them. It is one of the easiest things to squelch by unthinking big people. Children are natural collectors of anything and everything. The spontaneous child will come home with snails, caterpillars, lizards, flowers, old wrenches, nails, coins, and anything else that has a curiosity about it. You still have plenty of that urge within you. You can see it surface when you come upon a new animal at the zoo, or when you are out in the woods and run into an unusual bird or some rare creature. You want to check it out, to examine it and learn as much about it as possible. Perhaps you halt these urges, but nevertheless they are there, and being a happy person and more childlike involves letting yourself have healthier feelings of spontaneity in every area of your life.

The child inside of you hates organization and planning when it becomes obsessive. The constant analyzing, trying to figure out the why, persistently going over life's game plan, are all anathema to your natural self. But you continue to do it because you've come to believe that you are supposed to think and behave this way. If you have a completely planned-out life, knowing where you are headed with all of your goals spelled out, and you are obsessive about organization, cleanliness, and orderliness in your life, then you have not only forgotten how to be a child, you've stifled that wonderful little person inside of you.

During the holidays, you can go to work on eliminating some of the super-organizational behavior that infects so much of your adult life. You can eliminate the need to have the entire holiday season run on a schedule. You can shed some of your compulsive neatness by allowing more freedom in the house during this special time. You can get rid of your own timetable and instead stop to enjoy what is happening in your home. See what gives the most pleasure for all concerned, rather than attempting to constantly foist your traditions and routines on everyone. In other words, just let the holiday season unfold and happen as it will, rather than planning every detail and making yourself miserable when things are out of kilter.

As you can learn from a child's appreciation of the holidays, so can they and others learn from the special qualities that you bring with you. As you begin to think about making this the best holiday season possible, ask yourself what are the most important gifts you can give to your family, especially your young children. If I could create a perfect shopping list, it would include presents that you will never find in a shopping center or mail-order catalog. As you complete your shopping lists, think about giving some of these as well, and I assure you that you will have the best holiday season you've ever imagined.

▪THE PERFECT GIFTS FOR THE HOLIDAYS

Give these gifts to those you love:

▪ AN UNQUESTIONED ACCEPTANCE OF EVERYONE AS A VALUABLE HUMAN BEING. Show those around you that they are loved for who they are, not for what they do or how much they please you. Show them that your love for them is not based on their performance, meeting your standards, or obeying your rules.

▪ SHOW BY YOUR EXAMPLE THAT SEEKING APPROVAL IS NOT NECESSARY. Give the gift of self-confidence-building by clearly understanding and accepting that no one can be approved of by everyone all of the time, and that when one encounters some dis-approval, one need not feel immobilized or upset.

- **SHOW THAT FAILING IS NOT ONLY ALL RIGHT, BUT SOMETIMES NECESSARY.** Give the gift of being a person who is not afraid to fail. Show that you are willing to try new things and fail a lot on your way to becoming proficient at anything. Don't be alarmed when others experience failure, and help them to accept it as a necessary step toward growing.

- **SHOW OTHERS HOW TO ENJOY THE PRESENT MOMENT.** Give the gift of their own lives, to be enjoyed one day at a time. Allow others to be children, to love being where they are rather than always hurrying to the next place. Give them a present of the present, and accept them as whole and complete now.

- **SHOW THEM HOW TO AVOID WORRY.** Give them a gift of a worry-free life by not being a worrier yourself. Show others that you will tackle the problems you have, but that you refuse to sit around and just worry.

- **SHOW THEM HOW TO AVOID ANY LABELS AND ROLE STEREOTYPES FOR THEMSELVES.** Don't let them become individuals who label themselves as girls, boys, intellectuals, athletes, or whatever. Give them an example of a person who is not slotted into any compartment. A person who is just as comfortable sewing or playing touch football, crying or being brave, cutting the grass or doing the dishes. Give them the gift of the freedom to be anything, rather than limiting themselves in any way by nonsensical labels and roles.

• LET THEM WELCOME THE UNKNOWN. Encourage them to grow by giving them the gift of risk taking, exploration, and adventurousness in life. Allow them to wander into unfamiliar terrain, to be adventurous rather than staying with the familiar and always opting for security. Let them be guided by their inner lights, rather than following someone else's directions and being safe, but unhappy.

• GIVE THEM A GUILT-FREE LIFE. Give them the gift of never having to feel guilty. Teach them to accept responsibility for all of their actions, but to avoid the immobilization that goes with avoiding responsibility in favor of simply feeling guilty. Don't tell them to feel guilty about not pleasing you, but instead, show them that pleasing themselves and not hurting others in the process is the way to a happy life.

- **SHOW THEM HOW TO AVOID BEING DISHONEST.**
Give them the gift of total self-honesty. Let your re-
lationship be based on openness and not fear of re-
vealing yourself. Be an example of someone who
doesn't need to be a fraud, and reinforce the impor-
tance of truth as the only way to fulfilling relationships.

- **SHOW THEM HOW TO BE FULLY ALIVE.** Give them
the gift of being a person who can sparkle and appreciate all of life. Allow for new adventures, laughter, fun, creativity, and trusting your own inner
signals in all that you do. Teach them the funda-
mental truth of relying on one's self for happiness
and being able to bring happiness to virtually all circumstances, rather than trying to find happiness
outside of yourself.

Indeed, the holidays are for children, but you can
make this the best holiday season you've ever experienced by becoming more childlike yourself, by adopting new and more self-enhancing attitudes and
behaviors toward the holiday season, and most important, by giving the gifts of being fully human to those
whom you love. All of the nuisances, crass commercial
aspects, the tiring activities, can be discarded in favor
of your becoming a child again—not only for the enjoyment of those holidays, but even more important,
for the total enjoyment of your entire life.

TWO

Make This Your First "No-Limit" Holiday Season

Make up your mind right this minute. This is going to be your greatest holiday season ever! You are going to have a sensational time this year throughout the entire festive holiday period. No hassles, no headaches, no depression, and most important, no holiday blues. This is not only going to be your first stress-free end-of-the-year celebration, it is going to surpass your wildest expectations about what a holiday season can be. You are about to embark on—in a word—your very first *no-limit* holiday.

Please note that this is not a chapter about avoiding the holiday letdown, or how to eliminate the seasonal blues. The focus is not on how to avoid anything that is negative. Instead, the emphasis here is on being positive, up, full of life and fun in a season that is supposed to bring out the best in us, rather than do us in. The truth is that this time of year offers us a wonderful opportunity to rekindle the spirit of love and living life to the fullest. Right from the very beginning, you must think of the limitless potential that this season offers you in the way of improving the quality of your life and the lives of those around you. The emphasis here is going to be on having no limits on what you can get out of these holidays. So put on your positive eyeglasses, and for a few moments look at the upcoming days and weeks with this new vision. You are fully resolved to make this a no-limit holiday, and it all begins with your changing around those old attitudes and beliefs about the negative side of this glorious season.

If you have ever experienced a letdown at this time of the year, you know how immobilizing that can be. The important thing for you to keep in mind is that there is nothing inherently depressing about the holidays. Any down feelings that you have are a result of your own thinking apparatus. If you anticipate that things will be depressing, you will rarely disappoint yourself. So you mustn't blame the calendar for your down moments. You must look within yourself and resolve to have a positive attitude, regardless of the tasks that lie ahead or the fullness of your holiday schedule. Put a sign on your bathroom mirror that says very emphatically NO ONE IS GOING TO RUIN THIS HOLIDAY SEASON FOR ME . . . ESPECIALLY YOURS TRULY! That kind of a reminder will put you on the right footing for a no-limit celebration.

If you have your expectations set on positive, now you must take a look at how to keep this kind of a holiday spirit intact. Here are a few suggestions that will help you to rearrange your stressful attitudes about the holidays. Then, when you get these new strategies in focus, and remember what I said in Chapter 1, you can use my inventory of handy techniques for making this a different kind of holiday than any you've ever experienced before.

The attitudes in the right-hand column will help you to take the pressure off yourself and focus on having a stressless holiday season. But when you approach the entire process of holiday celebration with the attitudes conveyed on the left-hand side of the table, you place limitations on yourself before you even begin. These negative stressful attitudes are what I call a *many-limits* approach to the most beautiful time of the year. The limits placed on yourself can create anger, frustration, pain, illness, fatigue, unpleasantness, and worst of all, an inability to enjoy anything associated with the holidays.

STRESS-FREE ATTITUDES TO WORK ON
FOR THE HOLIDAYS

STRESSFUL ATTITUDES	STRESSLESS ATTITUDES
There are deadlines that I am expected to meet. Each event must be completed on time. I have to keep an eye on the calendar to be certain that everything is done when it is supposed to be done.	It doesn't really matter when everything gets done, as long as we are all enjoying what we are doing. If some things don't happen at all, it's all right. I am going to forget about all deadlines and simply enjoy each day to the fullest.
I have to get this whole season organized properly. I'll make a list and be certain that all jobs get accomplished. The organization of the work is really most important; otherwise things won't get accomplished.	I am going to stop organizing just for the sake of having order. I'll let up on the pressure of having to get everything organized. I'll let the holidays flow, rather than trying to make them fit into a fixed schedule. I will work at enjoying each moment, rather than planning the next one.

STRESS-FREE ATTITUDES TO WORK ON
FOR THE HOLIDAYS *(Continued)*

STRESSFUL ATTITUDES	STRESSLESS ATTITUDES
The most important part of the holidays are the specific events and jobs that ought to be associated with this time of the year. The presents, decorating, meals, and so on are what make the holidays a success.	People are more important than things. As long as everyone is happy and enjoying themselves, all of the events, tasks, and things are not really that important. I will watch the ones I love to see if they are happy and forget about all of the other rules.
We have a history of tradition surrounding the holidays, and I must make sure that these are maintained.	This year I am going to forget about tradition and simply approach the holidays from a perspective of spiritual fulfillment and enrichment for all of my family and friends. I am not going to do things simply because I've always done them. We can be free to decide.

STRESS-FREE ATTITUDES TO WORK ON
FOR THE HOLIDAYS *(Continued)*

STRESSFUL ATTITUDES	STRESSLESS ATTITUDES
I get nervous and upset when no one else cooperates with me and I am shouldering all of the responsibility for the holidays.	I will relax my expectations for myself and others this year. No angry outbursts, and if others refuse to cooperate, then we will scratch that activity from our holiday celebrations this year. I will not become unhappy or down because of the behavior of others.
How can I enjoy anything when I have so many things to do?	I am going to become more present-moment-oriented, enjoying each activity for itself instead of always thinking about what is ahead of me.

STRESS-FREE ATTITUDES TO WORK ON
FOR THE HOLIDAYS *(Continued)*

STRESSFUL ATTITUDES	STRESSLESS ATTITUDES
Everything seems to be work for me.	I am going to attack everything I do from the perspective of play and fun, just like I did when I was a child.

If you are determined to rethink your own expectations for yourself during the forthcoming season, may I suggest that you try on some of these new behaviors that might, in fact, add a whole new flavor to your holiday. These strategies for having a no-limit holiday are specifically geared toward enjoyment and living your life to the fullest during a period when many people find themselves overwhelmed by shopping, addressing cards, wrapping, cooking, decorating, and an endless array of other jobs. Test some of these out this year, and see if your holiday season doesn't reverse itself from many limits to no limits for a change. Please notice, too, that none of these strategies requires any large financial commitment from you.

▪ Some No-Limit Strategies to Try
This Holiday Season

▪ Share your holiday season with new immigrants, particularly those from countries that have no exposure to our customs. Virtually every metropolitan area or college town in our country has recent immigrants or foreign visitors. Make arrangements to have them come into your home and experience sharing something loving and beautiful with people from other lands.

▪ Remind yourself that the holiday season can be lonely for people who are without their families, or cooped up in nursing homes, prisons, orphanages, and other similar institutions. Make every effort to expand your holiday celebration by sharing it with others who are less fortunate. Take some baked goods to a lonely older person and share several hours with him or her. Contribute some toys for children or contribute to other holiday programs for the needy, and give of your time as well. Sharing with others in less fortunate circumstances is what the holiday season is supposed to be about. You remember "Peace on Earth and GOODWILL TOWARD MEN"; why not make this more than an empty slogan this year and see how much better you feel as a human being who is part of the solution rather than part of the problem.

• Instead of a tree in your home, consider mobiles of suspended ornaments or another original symbol that fits in with your own family philosophy of holiday celebration. You can start your own holiday traditions with homemade symbols that have meaning to each member of your own family, rather than following the older, established modes that have always been a part of the festivities.

• Arrange to exchange baby-sitting days with friends who have children so you have uninterrupted hours to work or relax. Have neighborhood children baby-sit while you are in the house so you don't have to entertain children all day long. In other words, give yourself permission to have some alone time during the most hectic time of the year. Having privacy is an important part of staying healthy. Without these private moments to collect your thoughts, you will begin to feel like a slave to your family, and before long resentments will build up. You must remind yourself that you, too, are entitled to some alone time, and that you are going to devise the necessary baby-sitting or house-sitting arrangements to ensure that you maintain a sensible perspective throughout this demanding time of the year.

· Make a sign-up sheet and post it prominently so family and guests will divide responsibilities for meals. Create a kitty for money to be spent on groceries or restaurants. This will take the pressure off you for all cooking and meal preparation and help others to assume more of the responsibility for this time-consuming activity. You must teach everyone in the home that you are not the family servant. This will only be accomplished by being firm and showing everyone how you wish to be treated, not by words and angry outbursts, but by effective behavior on your part.

· Remove alcohol from your holiday celebration as much as possible. Drinking tends to make others less concerned about holiday responsibilities and tends to create an "I don't care" attitude toward being responsible. Liquor can also make people lethargic and uncaring about the real meaning of the holidays. It is very difficult to have a strong sense of family togetherness or spiritual awareness when the adults are drinking alcohol. Provide a variety of beverages and don't push the hard stuff. Most important, don't drive drunk or let a drunk drive you.

· Try to overcome the "shopping center neurosis" that is so prevalent this time of the year. Shopping in crowded, busy stores can become a troublesome experience rather than the joyful act of giving that holidays symbolize. Instead of shopping under these conditions once again this year, consider giving family heirlooms now, when you can see them enjoyed. Write a pleasant note with something that you want your children to have that has been in the family for several generations. Explain the significance of the item (even if you are starting a tradition of your own) and you can be sure that they will treasure it longer than the expensive toy or radio. Items from catalogs, plants, fruit, museum reproductions, magazine subscriptions, gift certificates to favorite restaurants or theaters, car washes for a year, and the like are all excellent examples of nonshopping gifts that live a long time and convey love throughout the year.

- Allow your children to make the wrapping paper this year. (They love these kinds of chores and this frees you from extra work and expense.) Freezer paper and crayons, glue glitter, or any number of other supplies along with their unique imaginations give the children activities and personalizes wrapping. The gifts do not have to look any particular way under your tree.

- Tape-record elders' memories of earlier days (Christmas in the "old country" or Hanukkah in Israel or holidays on the farm) and give a cassette to the children or grandchildren. Perhaps you could interview your own parents and make reproductions that you and your children will treasure always. You might even play their remembrances at Christmas breakfast. And with today's modern video equipment, you could make a video recording of such an interview and keep it as a part of each holiday season.

• For relatives far away, take pictures of the children and title them "A Day in the Life of —." Tape or transcribe the child's remarks or descriptions with captions and give this as a truly personalized present. You can be sure that the recipient will treasure such a thoughtful holiday gift forever.

• Make a book of recipes for college students or newlyweds. "Mom's Pot Roast," "Grandma's Chili Sauce," "Aunt Louise's Fruit Salad," or "Sid's Brownies" to tuck into a kitchen towel or apron for a meaningful gift that can be enjoyed by all family members throughout the year.

• Set a limit of money to be spent on gifts and insist on everyone's cooperation. This removes financial pressure and allows for much more creativity in holiday gift giving. Those who feel a need to spend more can make a donation to the Salvation Army, Toys for Tots, or the Hunger Project.

- Try a "progressive" holiday party—hors d'oeuvres at one place, salads at another, entree at another, and desserts at the final stop. This will link up relatives and friends so that no one has extreme expense or time-preparation burdens. Be imaginative.

- Arrange a conference call through the telephone company. Plan ahead so everybody is prepared to share the opportunity to "be together," yet still is free to make separate holiday arrangements.

- If alone and depressed, volunteer at a hospital, bake cookies and make sandwiches for the police and firefighters who have to work and be away from their families on the holidays. Check with church groups for holiday meals and how to provide for the needy. In other words, stop feeling sorry for yourself whatever the condition of your life, and keep in mind that no matter how badly you feel, there are millions of people in the world who are much worse off than you are, and then vow to help at least one of them.

- Keep in mind that it's never too late to have a perfect holiday. Don't be depressed by memories of

DR. WAYNE W. DYER

past Christmases. Do it *now* the way you always wanted it to be.

- Give the gift of love every day of the holiday season, and beyond into the entire season of life. . . . Say it out loud, give them a hug, resist your resistance, and demonstrate that love.

- After a trauma (perhaps the death of a relative) have your first holiday celebration away. New surroundings provide less painful associations in the beginning. Try Christmas on a boat, the holidays in Colonial Williamsburg, Hanukkah at a resort, Christmas in the opposite climate from your home—the desert or the ocean or snow-covered mountains.

- Buy yourself a nice present and enjoy it throughout the year. Each time you use anything you've given yourself, you will remind yourself that you really deserve this kind of a treat. Perhaps you can take somebody to a movie you want to see, or take somebody out to dinner, or purchase a record album and play it at your holiday gathering. The amount of money you spend is not nearly as important as the inner satisfaction you'll receive from giving yourself the treat that you deserve.

46

- Give a promissory note or a contract to someone you love; a promise to an older relative that you will shovel snow or mow the lawn; a promise to bake a favorite bread or cookies for those who love your special treats; a promise to go to three performances with your grown daughter or your young son who loves the theater. These kinds of written promises, done up in your own fancy, personalized contract, will make the holiday spirit extend throughout the year.

These are some no-limit strategies you might try on for the holidays this year. Obviously, the list could be extended endlessly, with the only limits being your own imagination. This time of the year does not have to be celebrated in a certain way. There are no shoulds or have-tos, other than those you have imposed on yourself.

I strongly recommend you make a commitment to yourself that there will be no limits associated with this holiday season. Make a personal vow you will not have any stressful thinking or behavior to diminish this beautiful time of the year. Every time you find yourself feeling the pressure, or becoming a servant, or feeling depressed about the way things used to be, try imaging the word CANCEL like a huge rubber stamp on your mind. You will stamp CANCEL on any self-defeating image you place in your head. If you start to think "poor me" thoughts, you will CANCEL that thought for the moment and begin to think in some kind of a self-enhancing way. If you image an angry thought, you will CANCEL it with your rubber stamp and begin to think about how you can make this time of the year better for someone else right this very moment. The focus of all of your mental energy must be on positive channels instead of self-pity. This kind of thinking will ultimately become a habit, but it will only become a positive habit if you practice positive thinking when you are just beginning to get yourself down. This is the perfect time of the year to begin that kind of practice.

With your vow to make this your first no-limit holiday, and your catalog of strategies for thinking and behaving in more meaningful holiday ways, you will find each *present moment* of the holiday season to be something to savor and enjoy. And, after all, that's all any of us get during our short visit here, precious present moments to either live and cherish or waste away with negative thinking and actions. Every moment of our lives affords us a choice and the holiday season is no exception. Go for the no-limit choice and the results will astound you. This thing called life is a miracle, each and every particle of it, and the holiday season is a celebration of the miraculousness of it all.

THREE

Happy New Year!
How to Live in the Present Moment

F orget about those New Year's resolutions in which you decide on the first day of January how you will be conducting your life in September, some nine months later. Any resolution that involves you making decisions about long-range upcoming behavior is not only a waste of time, but it reinforces the self-defeating notion of living in the future rather than in the present moment.

This is the only day that you get. Period. You can resolve to be skinny when next July rolls around, or to quit smoking next month, or to write those long-put-off letters, or to embark on your overdue physical-fitness program by the end of this year. In fact, you can go about resolving until the cows come home, and you still have to live your life just like everyone else on this planet: that is—ONE DAY AT A TIME. Whatever it is you are making resolutions about for the future, keep in mind that you cannot do anything for a year because you are constricted by the reality system in which we are all living every day. Whether you like it or not, you can only live minute to minute. You can certainly use up your present moments thinking about what you'll be doing in the future, but that doesn't change the fact that you can only live in the now. The important questions to be asking yourself are "How am I going to use my present moments this year?" and "Will I waste them in reviewing to myself how I used to behave, or how I would like to behave in the future, rather than resolving to live each day to the fullest?" When you look realistically at the alternatives, you see very clearly that just like you did every other year you are going to be forced to live in the present moment. The choice you *can* make involves not using up those precious present moments doing self-defeating things such as living in the past, worrying about the future, or making resolutions for the entire year.

▪An Alternative to New Year's Resolutions

There is absolutely nothing neurotic about making plans and then proceeding to carry them out, and the New Year is as good a time as any to initiate a self-improvement program. But rather than making your plans for a full year, see if you can practice thinking differently about your ideas for changing yourself in a positive way. Decide very specifically what it is that you would like to change about yourself. If you have some goals in mind, vow to attack them in a day-to-day mode, rather than making it a year-long project. The reasoning behind this approach is really quite simple. Supposing you decide you want to lose twenty pounds, and your New Year's resolution involves eating no sugar for the rest of the year. Immediately you begin to think about how difficult this is going to be. Your mind starts working on ways for you to give up on this silly task, so you start thinking, "Wow, this is really going to be tough. I know I'm going to be craving some sugar before next weekend." With this kind of a mindset, you are already doomed to maintaining, if not adding to, your twenty pounds of excess baggage. And when you think about it, your mind is being very effective. Why should you want to do difficult tasks when you are much better equipped to handle easy ones? As soon as you make the task difficult (such as a year-long goal) then you set yourself up to give up on the idea.

What you can do is set up day-to-day goals for yourself, and then resolve to begin living this way for the rest of your life. Back to the twenty pounds you want to shed. Supposing you decide that you are only going to go one day without eating sugar or any fattening foods. Now you know that anyone can do virtually anything if it is for only one day, but you may believe that you are really only deceiving yourself, and you know you'll have to do it for a lot of days, and it is going to be tough, so why even try? This kind of self-defeating logic is the very thing you must learn to conquer. Remember this little piece of advice, which will be extremely helpful to you if you can incorporate it into your life: When you go for one whole day without eating sugar (or not smoking, or being assertive, or any other new behavior), you are a *totally different person* at the end of that day. What you must learn to do is let the *totally different person* decide on the second day whether he or she wants to do it again on this new day, rather than letting the *same old person* decide today that it is only going to be difficult in a couple of days anyhow, "so what's the use." Always let the *new you* make the decision, and then you'll be living your present moments.

You are aware of how easy it is to give up on a resolution, and you may have attributed this to some character flaw or personality weakness. Not so! You give up on your resolutions because you are resisting the absurd notion of trying to live your life in long stretches, when it is patently impossible to do so. If you can do it in daily sequences then you will not be deceiving yourself at all. It is simply a matter of asking yourself at the beginning of the day, "How do I want to conduct my life today?" Then very directly begin to carry out those goals for the day. When you get good at living your present moments one day at a time, you'll find that you've removed that onerous "global goal" from your life, and you'll also see yourself changing right before your own surprised eyes. Remember, anyone can do anything for just one day, so tune out the sentences that keep you locked into your old self-defeating ways.

• SOME THOUGHTS THAT KEEP YOU FROM LIVING IN THE PRESENT MOMENT

If you ever use any of these thoughts or sentences in your life, then you are going to remain exactly the way you are today, and you will never be able to enjoy your present moments.

- **I CAN'T HELP THE WAY I AM.** This kind of logic ensures that you will never change, and that you can't live today the way you would like to because, after all, you just can't help the way you are.

- **I'VE ALWAYS BEEN THIS WAY.** And the neurotic conclusion is you are always going to remain that way. Just because you've always been a certain way is not a justifiable reason for remaining the same, unless of course you are looking for an excuse to keep from taking on new roles in your life.

- **THINGS WILL GET BETTER IF I JUST WAIT THEM OUT.** Things never get better by themselves. If you want things to get better, then you are going to have to grab hold of yourself in this moment (today) and do something constructive. By being alive in this moment you'll ensure that things will improve, but by using this tired old lament, you'll be hauling out another excuse to keep you from present-moment action.

- **SOMEDAY THE KIDS WILL APPRECIATE ME, EVEN THOUGH THEY DON'T TODAY.** This is future-oriented thinking of the worst kind. You are sacrificing yourself now for a future time when your children will finally come around. If you want to be appreciated, do something about it today. Stop the foolishness of picking up after everyone, being the children's little slave, or whatever, in the name of a future appreciative reaction from them. If it hurts now, take corrective action now, rather than waiting.

▪ THINGS WILL NEVER BE AS GOOD AS THEY USED TO BE. These are the good old days, and you cannot recapture any days out of the past. Forget what is over and get on with living today. You have control of the images that are in your head, and any thought that keeps you reminiscing, in lieu of living today, is one to put out of your head forever. . . . One day at a time!!

Similar sentences that keep you out of present-moment focus include:

▪ You have to suffer now in order to get your reward later.

▪ He'll come around someday if only I am patient and put up with his abuse.

▪ You can't expect to have everything you want.

▪ You must always be cautious and save for the future.

If you look very carefully at the logic inherent in these utterances you will see you have bought into a conspiratorial kind of logic that has you believing it is healthy to postpone your gratification in the name of being unselfish, careful, or "right." But you must take a more skeptical look at this kind of thinking and begin asking yourself exactly what the nature of your reality is all about. If you don't take advantage of today, when will you ever be able to do so?

I know of many people in their eighties and nineties who refuse to spend their money because they are saving it for their old age. And what happens? They die and never use it, passing it on to anticipating relatives or having it eaten up by inheritance taxes. When does your present moment arrive in which you can do things for yourself in order to have pleasure in your life? If you don't get into the habit of living in the present, then you'll never be able to do it, and you will accumulate a nice tidy sum of money, collectibles, and miseries, which you'll pass on to the next generation.

■ THE VICIOUS CIRCLE

Henry David Thoreau once said, "The mass of men lead lives of quiet desperation." There is still a lot of truth in this nineteenth-century observation, and the vicious circle that produces quietly desperate people operates something like this.

At point one on the circle is the inclination to *idealize*: to be thinking about some future event and using up the present moment in anticipation of that event. Things will be great—"when I get to the dance next Friday, when I graduate, when I get married, when I get that promotion, when we have our first child, when we get our new house, when we get that bonus, when the holidays arrive, when our friends arrive from out of town, when they leave, when I pass my examinations," and on and on the idealizing goes. We are always anticipating something in the future and using up the present moment planning, figuring, hoping, wishing, dreaming, or whatever, always about a future time or event.

As the circle continues to point two, the obvious result of future-oriented idealizing is the logical *frustration* that follows such thinking. "The dance wasn't really that great, graduation was a bore, the honeymoon was over right after the wedding ceremony, I spent the bonus even before I got it, the holidays were trying and I couldn't wait for them to end." The message is clear. When you are accustomed to idealizing and using up the present thinking about the future, then when that future becomes today, you *have* to be frustrated because you have no preparation for enjoying the now.

The third part of the circle is a sense of *depression* that results from feeling unfulfilled. You've become enthralled with the future and allowed yourself to be let down by idealizing so much. Because you didn't know how to grab ahold of the now and live it, you feel depressed and demoralized. So what do you do? You idealize again and start the process all over, with the end result being that you fit neatly into Thoreau's notion of living your life in quiet desperation. The only way out of this trap, which immobilizes countless millions of people, is to straighten out that circle and begin living your life fully today.

I am not suggesting a life-style that is irresponsible and pleasure-seeking at the expense of anyone who gets in the way. What I would like to remind you of is that whatever you do in your life, and no matter how much you may protest, you must still live in the present moment at all times. The question is not whether you choose to live in the moment, but in how you choose to utilize the moments.

•LIVING IN THE PRESENT
TO DISCOURAGE UNHAPPINESS

If you examine any kind of personal unhappiness or self-defeating behavior you will find a solution to the problem in *becoming more present-moment-oriented.* If you suffer from depression you will discover that it is almost impossible to be depressed when you become busy in any present-moment activity. You will often discover that illnesses, fatigue, insomnia, and many physical maladies disappear when you really become involved in living your present moments, and that they will only persist as long as you are willing to use up your present moments thinking and complaining about your various ailments.

Undoubtedly you have had the experience of finding yourself so busy or excited by a project that you literally sent away a cold, or you have become so involved in an activity that you forgot about being tired and lived for days on your natural high. Often, when you take on an important job or task, you become so intensely alive that you just don't have time for any unhappiness or sickness. This very kind of experience, if you can make it a regular part of your life, will get you into the kind of present-moment living I am advocating.

The next time you are feeling sorry for yourself,

begin to assess how you are using up that particular moment. You'll very soon see that your mind was a flutter of thoughts that were reminding you of how badly you had been treated, or was filled with worry about some future catastrophe, manufactured in your mind, and you were letting this moment go by, chalking it up on the liability side of your personal life ledger.

When you become really proficient at living in the present moment, you'll see that most of these problems will genuinely begin to disappear. In fact, they'll have to go away, because most problems are not really problems at all, but simply a matter of attitude toward a given life condition. The problem part is about 95 percent in the mind and 5 percent real. When you train your mind to be here and enjoy this moment in a way that is healthy for you, you won't have room for all those ominous thoughts that take you away from being here now in the present moment. See how simple the logic is?

▪ DESTROYING STRESS-PRODUCING MYTHS

As a child you were constantly being reminded that you weren't grown up yet, that you had to wait until you were bigger, and that you weren't really whole now, but if you did everything right you would grow up and become an adult. In other words, you were not complete but on your way to becoming complete, sort of like being an *apprentice person*. You very likely carry over many of these same kinds of feelings into your current life. Of course it is only a true picture if you decide to make it true. Just because a person is young or small does not make him or her incomplete, unless you believe that to be true and then set about convincing the young person of your convictions. The truth is that we are complete at all moments in our life. Because we are always in a state of change, each moment simply represents a different opportunity for experiencing the moment in a unique fashion. The fact that you are going to be older next year does not mean that this year doesn't count. But that is the logic most children are exposed to in their earliest years, and ultimately that myth carries right on into adulthood, and people have a great deal of difficulty in seeing themselves as complete, whole, and even perfect in this moment.

You must slay this demon of incompleteness if you are going to get on into present-moment living. Always consider this moment as one to experience fully and you are entitled to do just that. Certainly you are going to be growing, changing and developing many new and different skills and attitudes as you get older. But this is not necessarily a logical reason to avoid the enjoyment of these moments; instead it seems like a rational reason for saying to yourself, This is the only day I have for myself at this age, in this time, today. So why not grab ahold of this moment and live it, rather than putting off my fulfillment until I'm more complete?

The problem with the "Incompleteness Doctrine" is that you never really get to be a whole person, despite your age. The process becomes bigger than the goal of completeness itself. Consequently you become enmeshed in always thinking ahead to a future developmental stage—until you are ninety, at which time you begin to review the good old days. The present never arrives for these conditioned postponers of life. Don't let yourself fall into that trap, which is a leftover from your early days when big people were able to really manipulate you with that absurd logic.

The second of these deadly sickness-producing myths is the idea that hedonism or pleasure-seeking is somehow a bad trait to acquire—the point of view being that we should seek out pain and suffering in order to be good people. The avoidance of living in the present moment can be traced directly to the multitudinous admonitions: . . . Postpone your gratification . . . Save for a rainy day . . . Be very careful . . . Don't spend all of your money on things for today . . . Sure, school is boring but it will pay off someday . . . If it feels good, don't do it . . . Wait until you are married, or grown up.

Let's set the record straight right here. Pleasure is terrific and you should try to fill your life with as much of it as you can get. No conditions, no apologies, a simple fact. Pleasure is to be sought out and pain to be avoided. Do you get mad at your plants because they stretch toward more sunlight? Why do they do that? Because sunlight feels good and encourages growth they instinctively seek it out. Do you discipline your pets when they seek to eat, or sleep, or romp? Why do they do all of these animal things? Because they feel good, and all animals know instinctively to go after pleasure and avoid pain.

This is not in any way an endorsement of grabbing your pleasure at the expense of others; I am not suggesting that people be crass or vicious in their pleasure-seeking. You must destroy the idea once and for all that you are being bad if you are seeking out pleasure. Your work ought to be fun. Schoolwork ought to be enjoyable for students, not some dreary exercise in plodding through painful learning experiences.

Life does not have to be full of misfortune, suffering, drabness, or misery. It does not have to be grim in order to be important. You are entitled to have every experience be one that gives you joy, and if your life experiences don't provide pleasure for you then you will be a much healthier person if you seek out that pleasure and do everything that you can to avoid suffering. While you don't have to develop a phony sense of excitement about changing dirty diapers or emptying the garbage, neither do you have to be immobilized by these routine tasks. You can resolve to do them cheerfully and then get on with enjoying your life.

If you decide to believe that pleasure-seeking is not a vice and indeed something that you want for yourself, then you will also have to decide to get more into the present moment, particularly during the holiday season, and stop all of the needless worry and guilt that use up your moments as a substitute for pleasure. By seeing yourself as complete in this moment and not *on your way* to anyplace, and by giving yourself permission to have pleasure now rather than waiting for it at a later stage in your life, you'll have incorporated the two necessary attitudes to help you achieve self-actualization in the present moment. Below are some specific kinds of strategies that you might find useful in changing from a postponer and other-moment person to a NOW human being.

■ SUMMARY:
STRATEGIES FOR DEVELOPING
PRESENT-MOMENT AWARENESS

▪ First, and above all else, remember that you are in control of all thoughts in your head. When you are using up your present moments to worry about the future, constantly reviewing the past to come up with how you "should" have done it differently, or contemplating disaster with morbid thoughts, remind yourself that you are wasting this particular present moment. Practice *canceling* out those thoughts for a few minutes at a time and vow to yourself that you are going to enjoy the next five minutes regardless of what has previously transpired or what you think is about to happen. Remind yourself of the folly of wasting your present moments on mental activity that focuses exclusively on your past or imagined future. All of your thoughts about what you should have done, or how terrible things were in the past will not change one tiny slice of the past. Similarly, your worry about the future will do nothing to make it work out better. Once you begin to talk to yourself about the foolishness of torturing yourself in the present with other-moment thoughts, you'll get on with what is required to get out of those habits.

• Remember that habits are changed by practicing new behavior, and this is true for mental habits as well. The only reason you've become a procrastinator or a worrier (and therefore someone who does not live in the present) is you have trained yourself to be that kind of a person. By practicing new thinking in five-minute time blocks, you'll soon begin to master the art of present-moment living.

• Do an honest assessment of your "problems." You'll very likely discover that almost all of your problems are really in your head and not located in reality. If you have a shortage of money in your household, that is one thing, but worrying about it, fretting all of the time, nagging yourself and others, and always thinking about your impending bankruptcy are all mental-attitude problems. You can spend your time coming up with solutions rather than endlessly carping about the "problem," and you'll be behaving in a constructive manner. Virtually all problems are way overplayed in your mind. You must remember that your mind is your own and you're going to work at letting yourself BE HERE NOW.

• Try this exercise. Wherever you find yourself located at the moment, begin to look at your entire surroundings in a new light. Try to drink in as much of your life space as you possibly can. If you are on a street corner, rather than simply passing it by, stop for a minute and see how much you can really observe. Look up and check out the architectural design, notice the faces on the people who are passing, observe in detail the beauty of the tree and how it is growing, the colors, the textures, the odors, the cloud formations, the anguish on some faces, the hurried pace of this man. There are literally thousands of things to observe in every life-space moment if you retrain yourself to behave in this manner. You did this as a child when you would go into the woods. You would sit down and be captivated by a caterpillar. You knew how the flowers grew and what every single weed looked like. You observed the colors, the insects, and everything there was to experience. Now, as an adult, you simply walk (or drive) past the woods and say, "Look at the woods." As we have seen, becoming a little girl or boy again can help one appreciate all of the things life has to offer. If you do this often enough it will become a habit, indeed, a habit that will facilitate your being alive in every moment of the year after the holidays are over.

• Begin an attitude-redevelopment plan for yourself in which you determine to practice enjoying everything that you do. You can change around your mental notions about whatever tasks are a part of your life. Instead of having a sour attitude about a given activity, try seeing the positive side to your behavior, even if it's only for a few minutes. If you are saying to yourself as you read this, "Oh sure, that's easy for him to say, but he doesn't have my life to lead," I can assure you that you are right, but so what? Stop being right and disposing of all suggestions to make your life happier, and ask yourself what you are getting out of defending your miserable attitude toward some of life's responsibilities that you have chosen to take on for yourself. The point is that no amount of your defending your unhappiness by comparing yourself to others will do anything to make your life better. And that is why I'm writing this book, to help you to help yourself to a happier life, in the holiday season as well as the rest of the year.

• Get rid of your long-range goals and try to become specific about what you want today. Decide on one thing that you would like to have for yourself today. For example, don't state that you are going to get yourself into topnotch physical shape this year. That is far too long-range a goal, and an easy one to discard in favor of the more flabby lifestyle that you've become accustomed to. Instead, say, "Today I am going to walk two miles and do ten sit-ups." Then carry out this assignment and forget about what is going to happen six months from now. Before long your body will want more of that healthy exercise and you will just naturally upgrade your daily requirements. But do it—something, anything—today, and work at keeping it a daily, rather than a long-range objective beginning on January 1.

• In addition to keeping your goals in a short-range, daily mode, you must also keep them specific rather than global. It is common to hear people say, "My goal is to find myself," or "My goal is to improve myself." When you state your life objectives in these amorphous terms, you are not really saying anything. Instead, get specific with your objectives. Talk in terms of reading one new book, or writing one letter. Think about standing up to a pushy relative just once, rather than setting a goal to become "an assertive person." When a goal is global and general it is virtually unachievable, so you set yourself up to fail before you even begin.

• See if you can stop focusing so much on what the holidays used to be like. In conversations try to talk about a "now" rather than always being nostalgic. While it is fun to reminisce, it can also become a means to avoid your present moments if it gets carried to an extreme. Create tomorrow's holiday memories now, rather than using up this now to re-hash those golden oldies.

• Create a self-improvement agenda for yourself and practice carrying it out on a regular basis. Make a list of some books that you've always wanted to read but have never gotten around to. Include some classics, contemporary novels, nonfiction, and so forth. In addition, detail some of the places in your own town that you've never seen. Add to your agenda people you really want to get to know better.

What new activities such as tennis, racquetball, backgammon, horseback riding, sailing, jogging, and disco dancing have eluded you to date? Include these as well. Have you wanted to write a children's story? A magazine article? Compose a song? Fly in a small airplane? Go parasailing, waterskiing, cross-country skiing? Put on your agenda whatever activities you've always thought about but never included.

Add anything else such as taking a cruise, volunteering at a nursing home or mental hospital, bicycling ten miles, swimming a mile, eating in a Greek restaurant, or whatever. With this kind of a self-improvement or self-enjoyment agenda, you can check off the things that would help you become a more present-moment, alive person during the course of the whole year. Include activities with your family, gourmet meals, new sexual frontiers, traveling, discussions of poetry, quiet moments together, and the like. You can use this agenda, adding to it as you go along, to help you live more fully in your present moments.

• Treat yourself, and *everyone* you encounter, as whole rather than as apprentice people. Forget about what you are growing into and live your life one day at a time. Don't remind your children that they are only little and young now and on their way to becoming big and old. Enjoy them for what they are today and don't put that future orientation into either your life or theirs.

• Rid yourself of a lot of mundane chores that are not really that important. You don't have to spend endless hours doing housework or yardwork, or slaving over financial records or meals. It is not necessary to have laundry as a regular part of your life, particularly as your children grow older. Any child over the age of seven ought to know how to wash laundry and dishes, clean, and do any other chores, and these responsibilities can be shared by everyone, including men. When you fill up your life with activities that offer you little in the way of excitement, and then you justify this by saying that it has to be done, you don't give yourself the time to take more advantage of your present moments. Become more efficient and less fastidious about those necessary chores, and spend more time in making your life a pleasure. Believe me, everyone concerned will be the better for this kind of a decision. You'll like yourself better, and consequently you'll be a better person as well.

· Eliminate procrastination as a life-style by attacking it today. Instead of talking to yourself about what you are going to do next week or even tomorrow, simply use up the time that you would be thinking about it to start one task. Begin the letter that you've been putting off—don't say you'll finish it, just write the opening paragraph. Once you begin, let the new person who is not procrastinating make the decision about whether you'll finish the letter. This is the only way to attack procrastination. For example, you can put this book down right this moment and do one sit-up, and then pick it up again. If you decide to do it, then you are behaving in a physically fit manner for that moment. Don't plan—just do it.

· Refuse to be put into any roles ever again, beginning right now. When you must fulfill a designated role you are then forced to live up to the role definition, which discourages you from being spontaneous and alive in the present. For example, if you see yourself as an uncoordinated, unathletic person, and everyone else has stereotyped you as well, then you can't allow yourself to be outside of that role. Hence, when it comes to being at the beach, or watching a ball game on the grass, your role keeps you from joining in on the fun.

• Resolve not to be seduced into things where you give up control of your life to others. You cannot enjoy the present moment if you are busy trying to make everyone else like you by being a good little slave, and simply going along. Let others make independent decisions and take constructive steps to make sure that you are doing the same. People respect you more when you operate from strength and self-reliance, as long as you are not pushing your beliefs on others or using others to achieve your goals. Be independent and quiet about your present-moment goals, sharing them when you choose to do so, but always keeping in mind that you have to decide on your life priorities, and that your life is too precious a commodity to be placing control of it in any other than your own hands.

• Forget about *escaping* to anyplace. Every place that you are *in*, in life, constitutes an opportunity if you decide to seize it. While it is always fun to go to new places, forget about the escape aspect. You can see each life experience as a new challenge, be you in Madrid, Milwaukee, or Madagascar.

- Simply refuse to use up a present moment in a hostile argument when you feel yourself being dragged in that direction. Remind yourself that it is your life, and that you are not going to use up this moment (the only one you have) in being upset, hurt, and depressed. When you refuse to argue with someone, you are teaching them that you have too much respect for yourself to engage in this kind of pettiness. Soon others will follow suit and you'll have made a big change in your life in terms of living in a fully functioning way NOW.

These are some suggestions that you can incorporate into your life to get on with living in the present moment. I have personally used all of these methods to keep myself alive and happy in my present moments. I have decided that no one is going to ruin this day for me, and I am full of resolve about that. I enjoy things like running on the beach, tennis, music, discussions with strangers, beauty, animals, and writing in the middle of the night. I feel that I do not need to explain my decisions about how I am going to live my present moments to anyone as long as I am making the decision to be a responsible human being. But *I* decide how I carry out those responsibilities, not anyone else. I believe that I must take risks, that I must have new challenges, and that I want to experience every moment I'm alive in as full and exciting a manner as possible. If others find this difficult to swallow, then I consider that to be their problem, since it is my life we are discussing.

I know that I have to live with myself, and that I must feel good about that self I am always with. I do not want to get to the end of my days and look back at having missed this or that opportunity. So I have vowed to be fully alive and see the world the way Whitman described it many years ago: "To me . . . / Every cubic inch of space is a miracle." I really believe in that philosophy.

I strive to be fully appreciative of all things and moments in my life. Not by thinking about it all of the time, but by being a doer and an activist. I love the sun—so I go out into it—no questions, no worries, no fretting about what I should be doing instead. Similarly, I enjoy the company of people who are excited about life, who are not inhibited and afraid to take risks. I seek out these kinds of folks, and simply "pass" when I run into complainers, whiners, or folks who want to drag me down.

Here is a beautiful poem, written by an unknown (to me) author. It sums up the contents of this chapter very nicely.

I THREW THE KEY AWAY

I have shut the door on yesterday
Its sorrows and despairs
I have locked within its glooms
Past failures and mistakes.

And now I threw the key away
and seek a sunny room
Which I will furnish with hopes and smiles
And fragrant springtime bloom.

No thought shall enter this bright room
That has a touch of pain
No impatience, unhappiness
Shall ever entrance gain.

I shut the door on yesterday
And threw the key away
Tomorrow holds no fear for me
Since I have found TODAY.

May you live a long and productive life, ONE DAY
AT A TIME!

FOUR

Liven Up Your Emotional Choices and Avoid the Holiday Letdown

This is the time for happiness, right? 'Tis the season to be jolly with lots of Ho Ho Hos, bells jingling, children smiling, and happy, happy feelings everywhere. You hear these sentiments in all of the music, view the beautiful scenes in store windows and holiday cards, see people celebrating the coming of the holidays, the New Year, families reunited, and note festive parties and exquisite meals. With this preponderance of "happy-time spirits" everywhere, one would think this would be the time of the year when people would forget their troubles, let their hair down, and really enjoy themselves. But this is not the case. The season to be jolly is hardly the way it is at all. In fact, the opposite is often true. People tend to increase their dependencies on tranquilizers. The number of episodes of depression rise significantly, and admissions to in-patient treatment centers and visits to psychotherapists show increases during and immediately following this season. Perhaps most shocking of all is that the suicide rate shows a marked upsurge at this time of year.

With all of the emphasis on festive celebration, it is ironic that people become more anxious and depressed now than during the rest of the year, which is supposedly full of dull routine and maddening sameness. It is not at all uncommon to hear people say, "I can't wait until the holidays are over and things return to normal," or "I hate the pressure of the holidays, I wish Christmas and New Year's would be banned." You do not have to join in on the big Holiday letdown; in fact, you can make this particular year-end celebration a beautiful, fulfilling experience if you guard against negativism and then vow to implement some specific strategies that will guarantee that you and your loved ones truly enjoy the holiday season rather than be victimized by it.

▪ WHAT TO GUARD AGAINST TO AVOID THE HOLIDAY LETDOWN

- First and most important, work on your own attitude. Begin to think positively about the experience and determine that no one else is going to bring you down this year. Attack each activity with a determination to not be *done in* by it. If you are in a crowded store, stop telling yourself that this is a terrible mob scene and that you have to be anguished by it. Slow yourself down and view it as a choice you have made, refusing to evaluate the situation in negative terms. Practice your thinking in daily moments and you'll see that if you refuse to be upset, and you're determined, nothing will succeed in bringing you down, because you can choose your emotional condition.

- Change your expectations. If you go into the holiday season with expectations of a bleak experience, then you will simply be participating in a self-fulfilling prophecy. Don't expect to be hassled or harried. Allow yourself some flexibility and new experiences. Do create new expectations. No one is going to aggravate you, the crowds will not get to you, it is going to be a pleasant experience. Once you eradicate negative expectations and substitute positive ones, you'll be on your way.

• Get all competition out of your holiday activities. You are not in a contest to have the most presents, the biggest party, the prettiest tree or decorations, the largest meal, and so forth. Forget what everyone else in the world is doing about the holidays and decide for yourself, on terms you and your loved ones set, what it is that you want during this season.

• Practice ignoring attitudes and behavior that you find objectionable. If other people want to turn the holiday season into a commercial activity, that is their business. Forget it. If you see whining, greedy behavior on the part of other children, or even your own, simply refuse to be drawn into an emotional upset by their actions. Often they use this kind of behavior as bait to see your reaction. If you simply ignore it and don't reinforce it, it will go away; and if it doesn't go away, at least you have put some control over your life by refusing to be dragged into an emotional upset because someone else decided to behave in an obnoxious fashion.

• Refuse to allow yourself to be lonely, even if you happen to be alone for the holidays. Loneliness is an attitude that can be changed, and aloneness is nothing more than a temporary absence of other people. If you allow yourself to indulge in self-pity or fantasies of how your holidays ought to (or used to) be and then permit yourself to become depressed, you will be defeating yourself and bringing on the holiday letdown. You can choose to think anything you want, so it is really pointless to dwell on painful thoughts. Once again, activity is an antidote to sour thoughts and sad feelings. Perhaps you can be of help to someone who is worse off. If you are unsure how to offer your time and attention, there are agencies helping children, the elderly, recent immigrants, the handicapped, or impoverished people. Religious centers and municipal organizations often are involved in holiday charities and would welcome volunteers. You can certainly be grateful for being alive, and practice some old-fashioned counting-your-blessings behavior. If you take charge of your mind and simply decide that you are going to enjoy this time of year, then no one else's behavior will ever bring you down. You can also view being alone as a choice, since you can get up and be around others, or if you are incapacitated, you can telephone people (including those who are in the business of helping people who are alone) and work at your aloneness rather than be immobilized by it.

• Don't allow yourself to be pressured or driven into high-anxiety states. If other people want you to behave in a rat-race style, then you can refuse to co-operate and remind yourself that you are not going to be a "wreck" this year. If your children expect you to take care of all their needs, and your parents expect you to do fifty little items for them, you can teach them all that it won't be this way. Announce calmly that you have plans of your own, then rein-force your message, not with words but with firm behaviors. Let them take on some chores. Don't tell yourself that if you don't have things a certain way that everything will be ruined. All of the pressure that you feel at any time does not come from any-one else. No one can pressure a person who refuses to bite on the bait. So be firm about your unwilling-ness to choose stress and you'll soon see that others will respect you.

• Stop thinking rigidly about the holiday season. We saw in Chapter 2 that you do not have to follow a plan you've always followed in order to have an enjoyable holiday season. Relax. A festive occasion calls for spontaneity rather than a rigid application of rules and rituals. There is no one right way to do anything, including celebrating. If the preparation requires too much of you, abandon it in favor of a less stressful activity.

• Be thoughtful about your holiday celebrations. Have a discussion with all family and friends involved. Ask yourself what it is that you want out of this experience, and then practice ridding yourself of work, pressure, and behaviors that are not constructive. If you want to bring the family closer together during the holidays and have them appreciate the true meaning of each particular holiday, then assess your current behaviors. Discuss your holiday activities, delegate authority, share in responsibility, and work at having no one scapegoat for all of the dirty work. By going after what you and your loved ones want, rather than doing what you're "supposed" to do, you'll not only rid yourself of the pain, but you'll be taking charge of your life in an assertive and exciting way.

· Watch out for taking on self-defeating habits. You get many excuses during this time of the year. Food is abundantly evident, drinks seem to be offered everywhere, smoking is a way of life, and people just consume more pills, including tranquilizers, antidepressants, sleep-inducers, and even simple over-the-counter drugs. You must guard against picking up these habits and then having to fight hard after the New Year to get back to normal. Often, getting back to normal means staying overweight, smoking more, or being more reliant on external antidotes in your daily life. You do not need to be drunk to be a celebrant, or to overeat simply because there is a lot of food. Be firm with yourself, and not only will you avoid the holiday letdown and the self-imposed guilt that comes with being weak, but you'll feel better about yourself for having resisted temptation and remained full of resolve about yourself.

Give yourself permission to enjoy this holiday any way that you choose. Just this year, give yourself some freedoms that you've never allowed yourself in the past. Give yourself permission to try new things, to establish your own traditions, and to stop being manipulated into all of the chores in the name of "it's your duty." You need not have even one moment of letdown this year. You can enjoy the holiday season from the opening day of all celebrations, including Christmas Eve, Christmas Day, Hanukkah, family visits, post-Christmas days, New Year's Eve and Day, and the days immediately following the New Year. Below are some specific ideas for how you can implement a stress-free, tensionless holiday season, and come out of this time period happy and free of anxiety.

▪ STRATEGIES FOR AVOIDING
THE HOLIDAY LETDOWN

• Delegate responsibilities and activities so that you are not taking on more than you could ever accomplish. Have a family meeting in which each person agrees to a portion of the necessary chores to reduce the workload on any one person. If someone fails to accomplish his or her end of the bargain, rather than becoming upset about it firmly remind the person involved. If he or she simply doesn't complete the task, then let the consequences of this behavior stand, with appropriate punishment, rather than assuming those responsibilities yourself. Thus, if someone doesn't go to the party store for soda pop and napkins, do without until the person responsible gets the message. You'll be surprised how people will be willing to contribute when they have behavioral evidence that you are not going to fill in if they fail to measure up.

• Do not assume responsibility for the entire household's holiday happiness. Take stock of yourself and do what you choose to do to make this a pleasant time. If there are some who simply refuse to appreciate what you are doing or who want to be grumpy, then ignore them. You'll soon see that most of their hurt feelings or sour behavior is nothing more than a strategy to get you to react. You can be kind, gentle, and understanding, but this does not mean that you must be upset or manipulated simply because others choose to be miserable.

- If you see evidence of greedy, whiny behavior don't reinforce it by constantly paying attention to it, or by getting angry yourself. Leave a room temporarily when you see behavior that you find objectionable, or simply refuse to participate in being a referee for every little holiday-season dispute. Once you have taught the members of your family that you are just not interested in being involved in petty arguments or infantile outbursts and that in fact you'll be leaving the scene when they crop up, you'll be helping them to understand your position, and you'll be teaching them to stop this kind of annoying behavior around you.

- Work minute by minute on your attitude. Push out those thoughts that will bring you down. Remind yourself that this is a highly active time for most of the children, filled with surprise and excitement almost daily. They, too, are unaccustomed to having this high-level excitement and newness in their lives, so they react with some behaviors that you find disturbing. If you give them a little of this understanding and delay any outburst of frustration, you'll be modeling the kind of behaviors that you want them to display. Postpone being angry because someone is talking too loud, and talk to yourself in soothing ways. This approach will serve you well throughout the year, but it is especially helpful in high-activity holiday times.

• Any task that you take on, such as cooking, wrapping, shopping, cleaning, arranging, chauffeuring, organizing, and so forth, should be viewed as a choice you have made. If you simply don't like the choice and are doing it anyway with accompanying hostility and upset, then work at developing alternatives. But if you are going to do these things, vow to do them with a sense of fun and enjoyment. Of course there are alternatives. You can forget the cleaning and stop putting starchy-clean demands on yourself, or you can get someone else to do it for you if you can't stand a little clutter. You can have someone else do the wrapping. You can announce that you will not cook every single meal and reward yourself with a Christmas dinner at a favorite restaurant. Remember, if you are going to do something, do it and enjoy yourself. If you simply can't enjoy yourself, then look for alternatives rather than suffering in silence. For example, think of holiday shopping as a challenging game with rules and strategies for winning your goal of completing your tasks quickly and smoothly. Give yourself mental points for not becoming unglued by clerks and fellow customers who are not enemies, just members of the opposing "team." Add to your score for getting out of the parking-lot traffic jam with your sense of humor intact!

• Start traditions that seem to make the greatest amount of sense to *you*. If you've always opened your gifts on Christmas morning, or decorated your tree on Christmas Eve, or gone to a nightclub on New Year's Eve, and these choices are fraught with tension or just don't make sense, then change this year. Do it the way you and your loved ones would enjoy the most. If you must sacrifice a night's sleep, or sit in a smoky room simply for the sake of tradition, then ask yourself why the ritual is more important than the person it is supposed to be serving . . . that is, YOU. Then start a new tradition. Open your presents when you choose to . . . get the tree when you can have the most fun out of it and enjoy it the most for everyone involved. If you've always invited the same surly relative over and he/she is always unappreciative, then stop it this year. Send a note with an explanation, and then carry out your new risk-taking behavior. You are not being bad, immoral, or otherwise Scrooge-like simply because you refuse to do things the way things have always been done and you or your loved ones refuse to be victimized.

- Vow to do things with your children that both of you enjoy doing together, rather than taking on a martyr's role. If you dislike playing certain board games, and your children received them for the holidays, this does not immediately oblige you to return to your childhood and play these games. (Of course if you like doing it, then by all means do so.) The activities that you participate in with your children should be mutually enjoyable. You can substitute going sledding or tossing a Frisbee for board games, and your child will enjoy it just as much. They will find other partners for their games, and you will be freed from feeling responsible for playing every single little game and looking at your watch to see when this will be over. Far better to do something that you are all enjoying than to be phony and pretend to enjoy doing something. Moreover, your children will see right through your feigned enthusiasm and feel even more resentment because you are telegraphing signals that you are anxious to get away from them.

- With your behavior, show visiting family members that you are simply not going to be manipulated with erroneous-zone behaviors such as guilt, worry, anger, or self-reproachment. First become an expert ignorer rather than be drawn into meaningless arguments. If a cousin, grandparent, or uncle insists on having you do something a certain way, and you don't want to, just continue on with your business and firmly inform him or her that you'll be doing things the way you choose to do them. People will respect your strength, but you must overcome your reticence about speaking up for yourself. If you believe in yourself and trust yourself to do things properly, then you don't need someone else (anyone else) telling you how to do it. When you get that unwanted advice or pestering, the only way to send it away is to ignore it, or to state firmly that you don't need help right now. Family members are the only ones who take attendance and grade you on your demeanor, dress, makeup, cooking, decorating. Some feel that by virtue of the fact they are related to you they can tell you how to live. With just one or two strong but polite interventions, you rid yourself of the internal upset, and you'll have a great feeling of accomplishment and self-respect, along with improving your holiday enjoyment immensely.

• Stop telling yourself that you must get ready for the next meal, or the next visitors, or the party next week or whatever. View the whole holiday experience as a moment-to-moment thing to be enjoyed.

For instance, buying and decorating a Christmas tree can be broken down into a series of present moments to enjoy—picking it out with the children or a lover, installing the tree, decorating it, putting the presents under it, enjoying the look and smell of it. Deal with each event as it arises and make it fun, and anytime future chores occupy your mind, push them out and deal with them when you are able to. Let people wait on themselves. Worrying about next Thursday's dinner while you are picking out a tree will not help you make the dinner any better, nor will it help you enjoy this moment.

- Get others creatively involved in the holiday activities. Let the kids wrap the gifts they are giving, even if the packages look somewhat disarrayed. It is better for them to feel a sense of pride in participating, than to have a perfectly wrapped gift. And it will free you from the responsibility of having to do it yourself. But avoid judging the finished product. Similarly, you can have them decorating the tree, or making salads, or doing any of the hundreds of chores that go with the holiday scene. What if the kids are in charge of Christmas dinner? Canned soup and peanut butter sandwiches served by candlelight with love and pride by small children is as grand a meal as roast turkey or prime rib. They may even enjoy their contribution enough to start a new tradition! But you must rid yourself of all perfectionistic ideas about how things have to look, and remember that the payoff is in the children's increased self-respect for having done something, rather than once again having watched while Mommy or Daddy did it and complained all the way through.

• Make a list of all of the things you dislike about the holidays, and see how easy it is to rid yourself of most of these bothersome tasks. Do you dislike sending out greeting cards? Then simply stop doing it this year. Do you hate Christmas pudding? Then leave it off of the menu, and see if the roof will really fall in. Do you hate all of those cheap toys that break after two days? Just don't buy them, and look for more effective ways to spend your money. The message is, if you really dislike it and it brings you grief, why are you doing it? Stop engaging in this self-punitive behavior and you'll discover that your holidays will improve and you will like yourself better for having kicked some old habits.

• Don't overspend and go into debt in the name of providing a nice holiday for everyone. The accompanying worry and ulcer-producing anxiety is never worth the price. It is not important to spend lavishly in order to show you are a loving person. All of those expensive gifts are almost always ignored after the first day, and you may still be paying for that moment of pleasure well into April or May. Be reasonable about what you spend, and tell those involved that you think it is foolish to go into debt for the sake of a well-stocked gift bag. People will appreciate your thoughtfulness when it is sincere, rather than when it is masked with high-priced items. You do not purchase love and friendship, and far too many people attempt to do just that with lavish spending. If you don't like the commercialism of the holidays, then don't join the very forces you find objectionable.

· As I discussed in Chapter 1, try to get your family members (and yourself) involved in making things for people, rather than purchasing them. A gift of a drawing, a piece of macramé, pottery, a wall decoration, a poem, a handmade greeting card, a photograph, a pillow, or anything into which human effort has been put will bring joy during the actual making of the gift, as well as in the giving. This technique of being involved in the gift itself will help immensely in avoiding the holiday letdown, because you'll feel a real sense of accomplishment and meaning in your life. Decorate the tree with handmade items, write poems to each other, and encourage other kinds of personal-touch activities.

• If you decide to purchase gifts, attempt to get things that have substance and will be personally meaningful to the giver and the receiver. Presents that reflect creativity include books, art materials, drawings, records, plants, animals, or building blocks. By being original and creative in your gift-giving you'll be helping others to grow and learn from your gifts, and you'll feel good about yourself as well.

• Provide for time with family members and other loved ones in which you share the real meaning of the holidays. Read aloud some of the passages from religious works or poetry and stories that are most meaningful to each person, by having individuals select what they would like to share with everyone else. Sing carols. Pray together and give thanks for having each other. Share with each person how you feel about him or her, have time for touching, holding hands, meditating, or just being together quietly. These are things that people always remember as they look back on their fondest memories—those touching moments at holiday times when love was shared in a unique way. If the holiday season is particularly religious in your own personal beliefs, then take time to talk about what is being celebrated, get the viewpoints of everyone involved, and discuss what it means to each person. Find out how people feel about the crass commercialism or the Christmas music. By giving yourselves some time to be tender and genuine, you'll infuse your household and your relationships with meaning, and you'll be doing something very positive in the way of eliminating any holiday letdown.

• Refuse to feel any guilt about having changed over the years. If you used to enjoy New Year's Eve parties and now you prefer to be at home with your family or alone, then stand by your convictions. You are entitled to change without explaining yourself or feeling guilty about it. Simply acknowledge that you are now different and that this is perfectly acceptable. (The reverse is also possible; you may wish to go out now, while you were once content to stay at home.) You are no longer in the nest, and your holiday behavior does not have to be the way it always was. But most important is that you realize you need not feel guilty about wanting things to be different, since this is a basic human drive of which you can feel proud rather than ashamed.

• If you are deciding to attend a New Year's Eve or other holiday party, do it on your own terms without having to become inconsiderate. First, make a real decision about whether you really want to attend; if the answer is no, then politely inform your friends that you won't be going, and don't fret about your decision. This is your life, and you have a right to refuse any invitation that comes along without feeling guilty. If you do attend, don't be shy about leaving when you want to go home. It is not necessary to punish yourself for the sake of doing what everyone else is doing. If they enjoy staying up all night, and you don't, then make this clear to all concerned. If your spouse wants to stay and you prefer to leave, this need not be a big issue. Simply arrive in two separate cars, or arrange for a ride home when you are ready to leave. Additionally, you can be assertive about your own party behavior as well. You can practice avoiding small talk and gossip by refusing to get seduced into conversations about drapes, or Mrs. Jones's current affair. When these topics surface, you can become quietly effective and just let your mind do what it wants to at this moment. The options available to you are multitudinous, from changing the topic yourself, to walking away, to greeting someone you didn't see earlier. You can be creatively alive in every life situation rather than sit there and be politely victimized. When drunks come around, you can move away. Never be driven home by someone who is drunk by whatever definition of drunk *you* choose to apply. No holiday party has to be unpleasant when you decide to attend on your own terms, and want to avoid being done in by anyone who you don't prefer around you. Make occasions fun, or simply ignore them, but don't be let down by holiday parties when you can make so many alternative choices for yourself.

• Try doing something new and different on New Year's or Christmas Eve. Look again at the options I presented in Chapter 2. Be exotic and creative with your plans. Have a winter barbecue at midnight in the snow, or go to the beach and run on the sand. With the entire family check into a motel that has an indoor pool and have a swim-in; arrange for several families to join you and make it an adventure. Perhaps you can have a backgammon or tennis tournament, a sensitivity session, go to a bowling alley, or engage in ANY activity that brings enjoyment. These kinds of activities are alternatives to the fancy overpriced packages that are offered in which you are jammed into a crowded, smoky room and given no individual attention for an entire evening, all in the name of holiday celebration.

• When the entire season is over, sit down, relax, and COUNT YOUR BLESSINGS. Remind yourself how nice it is to live in a country where you can celebrate a religious holiday, when in fact there are more people living on this planet who aren't allowed to do that. Remember how nice it is to be loved and to show that love to those around you even if it is only one person. Remind yourself about all of those who are in hospitals, old-age homes, mental institutions, and prisons. Try to visit them, or send a greeting, or give a little bit of yourself to someone less fortunate. Try donating some portion of your budget to those who need it the most, and see if it doesn't make you feel more complete as a human being.

These are some of the numerous techniques you can implement this season to avoid the typical holiday let-down that infects so many people at this time of year. You have choices in this business of holiday celebrations. The responsibility is always your own. This is a great time of the year. The true meaning of the holidays is one of joy, love, peace, and happiness. Why subvert the very essence of this beautiful celebration by thinking of it as something that you want behind you. The message is simple: Cultivate a childlike awe and appreciation for the holidays. Resolve to work on your ATTITUDE moment to moment. Share in the work AND the fun, avoid traditions that have become burdensome, be creative, and refuse to let the behavior of others affect your peace and enjoyment. In short, be yourself and be firm, and you'll have a joyous holiday.

This year it can really be the season to be jolly . . . but only with your cooperation.

Happy Holidays!

Here is an excerpt from REAL MAGIC,
by Dr. Wayne W. Dyer.
Available now from HarperPaperbacks
wherever books are sold.

When you are at purpose you are truly flowing with life, experiencing a kind of harmony that comes from not having to strive for something else. In short, you lighten up, figuratively and literally. This comes from the new knowing that enables you to go about your life's work free of worrisome thoughts. You sense that you are being watched over, and your actions come from this inner beatitude of rightness or centeredness. When you are acting out of that inner knowing which constantly reminds you that you are on purpose and that you trust yourself to act out of that purpose, the right thing is all that you can do.

The holiest book of the Hindu faith is called the *Bhagavad Gita* (the Song of the Lord). It is the story of Arjuna, the most renowned warrior of his time, and Krishna (God), who appears to Arjuna on the battle-field as Arjuna prepares to do battle. Krishna appears in the physical form of Arjuna's charioteer. In eighteen short chapters Krishna talks with Arjuna about the essence of being a divine and purposeful human being. This is the book on which Mahatma Gandhi modeled his life. Summarized briefly the Gita's message is: Behave in ways consistent with love and harmony and do not be attached in any way to the fruits of your labor. If you can attain this state of grace your life will become miraculously peaceful. Live your life entirely on purpose and renounce any and all credit that may come your way from your actions. Be consistently aware of the need to serve God and to serve others in any and all of your actions. This is the way of the miracle worker.

You may be thinking that this is a nice philosophy but one that is too simplistic in the dog-eat-dog, competitive world of the twentieth century. I acknowledge and respect your reservations. In fact, I lived with similar skepticism for the larger portion of my life. I had to go through suffering in order to learn life's lessons; I was totally focused on outcomes and was not a believer in matters metaphysical, nor was I interested in hearing about being detached from the results of my labors. I was in it for the results. I was focused on my destination, not the journey. The issues of my life concerned rewards, money, prestige and accomplishments. While I was certainly a "success" in conventional ways, I had no idea about going beyond these extreme indices, or about real magic. I can only say that miracles and real magic began to show up in my life when I got myself to purpose. Only when I stopped being concerned about what was coming to me was I able to be in a state of grace.

Here is a portion of a letter I received recently from a reader in Goodlettsville, Tennessee, that describes the experience of readiness to discover one's life purpose.

Dear Wayne:

As I sit by the fire in my den, my favorite
room, I feel so peaceful. All the usual things are
happening. Nine P.M., three children going off
to bed, my husband packing his bags for this
Phoenix trip, etc.

I sit here in the same room, the same clothes.
I know I look the same and yet I am not the
same person. I walk in the park across from my
home everyday and I listen to your tapes on my
Walkman. This is "my time," no phones, no
children, no noise, only your voice in my ears
and the beautiful park I have come to love so
much. I wonder why I didn't hear you ten years
ago, or five years ago when I was so unhappy. I
realized that I wouldn't have listened then, not
like I am listening now. Now is my time to hear
your message. Now I am truly listening and I
love what I hear. Tomorrow I will walk again
and probably finish hearing *The Awakened Life*. I
can just walk and walk and walk while listening
to you. It's so peaceful. Thank you from the
bottom of my heart. My life is now a miracle
unfolding everyday. I am on purpose.

For this woman, her life is a miracle yet nothing
outside has changed. The children, the chores, the job
are all still there, but she feels purposeful now and is

unconcerned about what the outcomes are going to be. This is the state I am hoping to help you to achieve.

Yes you can create miraculous changes in your life. Yes you have the power within you to manifest what may have seemed impossible only a short time ago. Yes you can know the meaning of real magic in your life. The setting for making this your reality is right there inside you. Get yourself aligned with your purpose. Discover the joy and peace of giving, not getting; of contributing, not acquiring; of doing, not competing or winning. Why? Because you can't really get anything. The message of your life is in what you give. You show up with nothing. You leave with nothing. All you truly can do with this life in form is to give it away. Purpose is always about giving. When you experience giving, serving, loving and promoting harmony you will feel the difference within yourself. André Gide summed it up so beautifully in his journal: "Complete possession is proved only by giving. All you are unable to give possesses you."

As you prepare for this exploration of real magic, you may be asking, "How will I do it?" "What if I need help?" These are sensible questions to which I want to help you find your answers.

▪ WHEN THE STUDENT IS READY

The first time I read the *Bhagavad Gita* it was as if a lightning bolt had illuminated my life. I had a similar experience when I read St. Paul's letters in the New Testament. Both of these wise and ancient works had been part of my library for over thirty years. I must have passed by them hundreds of thousands of times and probably had glanced through them as a young boy and a college student. Yet they had no meaning for me until I was ready, when they guided me to miraculous discoveries and helped me to get my life on purpose.

An ancient Zen proverb says, "When the student is ready the teacher will appear." When you are truly determined in your own mind to experience real magic and to live each day at purpose, you will be shown how to make it happen. Let's examine the four key words in this Zen proverb.

Student. Be a student. Stay open and willing to learn from everyone and anyone. Being a student means you have room for new input. When you are green you grow, when you are ripe you rot. By staying green you will avoid the curse of being an expert. When you know in your heart that every single person you encounter in your lifetime has something to teach you, you are able to utilize their offerings in a profound way. The ability to create real magic involves first of all being a student of life.

Ready. Be a willing student. Your level of readiness to grow and become your own miracle worker is simply a state of mind. As a student you know that everyone and everything is in some way your teacher. As a student who is ready, you are eager for what it is that everyone and everything has to offer you. The "wrong turn" leading to a new and unexpected place is an opportunity to grow. When you are a student who is ready, the stranger who talks to you about how he overcame his addiction years ago becomes a guide sent to you to help you cope with your own personal addiction.

When I was ready to leave alcohol behind me, truly ready, the teacher appeared for me in a meditation with these words, "You don't have to look any further. Do it now, you'll have all the help you are ready to receive." I had heard such words thousands of times, but my lack of readiness always interfered. This time, I was ready, and I was able to walk away from alcohol and never look back. Almost every magazine article I read in the next few days seemed to describe people finding the courage to leave alcohol and drugs behind them. Perhaps those same personal stories had always been there, but it wasn't until I was truly ready that they served as powerful reminders.

Ready means willing. Genuinely, authentically willing. When you are this ready, you will discover your own personal teacher.

Teacher. The teacher is everywhere. The assistance you need will be provided by the universe as soon as you convert your readiness to willingness. Once you are willing you will find teachers in every niche of your life.

The teacher might well be an experienced soul who is ready to assist and guide you to the miracles you seek. That person showing up in your life now, at the very time you are ready, might be construed as an accident or a divine break on your part. But that wise soul, in one way or another, has always been available to you. Your willingness makes the teacher able to assist you.

Teachers appear in various forms. Your teacher might be a tape that someone "accidentally" leaves in your car and that you "accidentally" play at just the right time. Last week you might have played it for two minutes and rejected the contents; now your willingness allows your teacher to be there for you. Your teacher might be a book or an article that a friend recommends. It might be your unplanned attendance at a lecture or a church service to which someone gave you their ticket because he or she had to be out of town; the message of the speaker seems to be directed specifically at you. Your teacher might be a child who takes you by the hand and asks you a question that you hadn't considered before, and your answer to the child is your answer to yourself. Your teacher might be invisible and show up as a thought that comes over you in a quiet, contemplative moment and encourages you to go in a certain direction now.

Hundreds of times people have come up to me after speaking engagements and told me how they "accidentally" showed up at one particular event or another and heard exactly what they needed at that time. For example, one woman was listening to a tape of mine while driving home. On the tape I was talking about the subject of "when the student is ready the teacher will appear." Suddenly, as she was driving by the Unity Church where I was to speak, she saw my name on the marquee advertising my appearance there that evening at 7:00. The time was 6:45. She pulled into the parking lot, purchased a ticket and attended the event. At the conclusion of the presentation she was shaking as she approached me onstage to tell me of this incident. "I've never driven home this way before, ever. I was driving my girlfriend's car and she happened to have your tape in her tape deck, so it was playing when I started the car. I've been thinking so hard about making some domestic changes in my life and after hearing you tonight I know that you showed up here in Chicago just so that I could hear you. I was ready and I was sent directly to hear you tonight."

This kind of story has been repeated to me hundreds if not thousands of times. "I needed to hear you today, and I know you came just for me." Yet I've been giving public seminars throughout the country for twenty years in virtually every major city over and over again. These people have seen the advertisements in the past, but their lack of readiness kept the teacher from appearing even though the teacher may have appeared right next door.

When you, the student, are ready and willing, the teacher will show up. You simply have to look around, open your new eyes and silently ask yourself, "Who is my teacher?"

Appear. The teacher is making an appearance in everything and everyone you encounter. As we've discussed, there really are no accidents. The universe is on purpose. When the teacher was there and you ignored that teacher, that was part of the perfection at that particular moment. The teacher, although there before you, wasn't there *for* you. That was then and this is now. Today, as you are getting your life to purpose and gaining the ability to make miracles show up in your life, you will recognize the teacher.

When the wounded, dying insect becomes your reminder of the need to be compassionate, the teacher has appeared. When the homeless person with his soiled presence and outstretched hand reminds you of your need to be merciful, the teacher has appeared. When the soldier loaded down with his instruments of death and ready to kill his assigned enemy reminds you of your need to send love and peace where it is most difficult, again, the teacher has appeared.

As you ask the question, "How will the teacher appear?" meditate on James Broughton's little ditty and you will have your answer:

> This is It
> and I am It
> and you are It
> And so is That
> and he is It
> and she is It
> and it is It
> and that is That

And that is that! The appearance of the teacher is everywhere, and without the teacher you will find yourself floundering.

Truly, no man is an island. We are all connected and we all learn and grow in this journey together. You will have all the help you need as you prepare yourself for miracle making and real magic.

You have now examined the idea of getting your life to purpose and setting yourself up for the assistance you will need in this endeavor. Yet the major premise of this book is that there is a realm of human existence that transcends what we have come to view as normal or possible. I am calling this dimension *real magic*. Once you genuinely feel yourself open enough to experience your own purpose for being here, and you have opened yourself up to receiving whatever divine assistance you may require by being a willing student, you will be ready to believe in your own capacity for becoming your very own miracle worker.

▪ BELIEVING IN MIRACLES AND REAL MAGIC

When I write about the world of real magic and miracles I am not referring to developing a talent for turning rocks into gold, raising the dead or commanding the seas to part. When I speak of miracle making I am discussing whatever you have considered beyond your ability to create for yourself because of limitations you believe you have. In later chapters I will describe the major areas of life where real magic is available. For now, I want you to cultivate the foundation for creating real magic in any area that you would like. If you have lived your life believing that certain accomplishments or levels of achievement were impossible for you, then first you must begin by examining your life focus and beliefs before attempting to implement any real magic strategies.

Getting your life to purpose and creating an openness to being assisted are crucial to becoming your own miracle worker. Beyond these qualities of purposefulness and openness there are guidelines for putting yourself in the proper mental framework. These beliefs, or "knowings," are necessary to help you go within and literally manifest what you have previously believed impossible. I will be alluding to these "knowings" throughout the pages of this book.

In my own life, I have had to travel through a sequence of steps, all within my mind, in order to be at the point where I can write that I feel confident in my ability to manifest what I can only call miracles. I call them miracles because only a short time ago, before I experienced this inner awakening, the things that I can now create and manifest seemed to be impossibilities. I offer these sequential steps believing that if it is possible for me, it is certainly possible for anyone else.

I am reminded of the words of Christ on his own miracle making: "He that believeth in me, the works that I do shall he do also; and greater works than these shall he do. . . ." Somewhere deep within you, you know that you have this kind of power. Even though you may not have an inkling of how to use it, or how to begin to tap into it, you still know that within each of us is a divine, invisible presence that has something to do with creating a state that can only be described paradoxically as real magic.

Christ went on to say, ". . . But ye shall know him;

for he dwelleth with you, and shall be in you." That's correct, *in you* is that magic invisible presence that I am writing about here. It is not something outside of you requiring a lifelong search to attain. It dwells within you, in that invisible part of your self, where the rules that pertain to the physical world simply do not apply. In your soul, your spirit or higher self, your mind or thoughts or whatever you choose to call it, lies that entryway to the world of real magic.

When you master the inner path of awareness presented in Part 1 of this book, you will not greet the application of this awareness with any skepticism, nor will you doubt that I am talking through that divine inner presence directly and unequivocally to you.

▪ Seven Beliefs for Manifesting Real Magic

I have identified seven beliefs, or knowings, that can help you tap the power of real magic. They are presented sequentially and once you find yourself with the internal knowing that comes from adopting these beliefs, you will be on your way to becoming your own miracle worker.

1. *There is an invisible but knowable life force within you.* Try cultivating an awareness of the invisible life force that suffuses all form in the universe, including your physical body. This is the same universal intelligence that directs a rose to be a rose, a beetle to be a beetle, the planets to align and move through space, and you to be you. It is without boundaries or dimensions in the same way that your thoughts, feelings, imaginings, dreams, fantasies and emotions are. This universal life force that is a part of you cannot die. Death implies an ending, and ending implies boundaries. For this first step, just know that this powerful, divine but invisible force is within you. Trust totally that it is there. It is in fact what allows you to perceive and experience your physical body and this physical world in which you find yourself temporarily housed.

2. *Your thoughts are something that you control and they originate with you.* In *You'll See It When You Believe It,* I wrote an entire section on the power of thoughts. Here I simply encourage you to realize that thinking is our way of processing and recording our human experience. Thought originates from within a nothingness inside of you and gives you your humanity. All of your past is in this realm of thought, as is your future. Your thoughts create your experience of your health, wealth and every detail of your world.

Ralph Waldo Emerson reminded us that "the ancestor to every action is a thought." You live the life you imagine you are living. When you stop imagining or imaging or thinking, you cease actively participating in your physical world. As a step toward the awakened life of real magic, you must consider how your thoughts have contributed to a nonmiraculous, limiting approach to life. Then you will know that you can also produce the opposite. If, in fact, miracles are available for anyone, you can be one of those people who experience them. But they begin in that ancestor to all of your actions, your thoughts.

3. *There are no limits*. All of the things that you have become convinced are limits are products of the way in which you have learned to think. You probably were taught that logic and scientific verification dictate what is possible and what is not. Before the invention of the microscope most people did not believe in the existence of microscopic life. People who believe only what they can see or prove scientifically are limited by the current level of sophistication of our measuring devices.

You know that at some future time we'll be flying from place to place on this planet in moments rather than in hours, and interplanetary travel will be a fact of life. The capability to do so is already here. That is, the universal force that is timeless already exists, only the technology is missing. Do you believe in this possibility now, or must you wait until the technology arrives before you can believe it? Only twenty years ago the idea of a remote control that would allow you to switch television stations was an impossibility. Renting a movie was unthinkable. Microwaving meals in a few moments at home was not at all a part of our consciousness. Although the capacity to create these miracles was available even at the time of Hannibal, the devices came along at their own pace. Be a person who accepts no limits in your mind. None!

4. *Your life has a purpose.* The entire universe is an intelligent system. The universe that is your physical body is a multitude of systems all functioning with amazing perfection, and it too is an intelligent system. The invisible parts of you, your thoughts and feelings, are also part of the system that is you. That intelligence is invisible and can be described or spelled in any way that you choose; thousands of terms have been invented to describe it. But the intelligence is not the label, just as the statue is not the saint and the menu is not the meal. You are that intelligence from which you can never separate yourself, and you have a purpose.

I have explained the necessity of getting your life to purpose and about getting yourself on that purposeful path. What I ask of you here is to simply know it. Know you have a purpose and you will be on your way to creating magical life in any and all areas of your choosing.

5 You overcome weaknesses by leaving them behind. You cannot outthink your weaknesses and limitations. You will not get yourself to the place of inner harmony necessary to create real magic by working hard to overcome your old self-defeating behaviors. What you can learn to do is leave that stage of your life behind you and walk through the gate into a new way of being.

This process of leaving behind old habits begins in your invisible dimension—that is, your thoughts. You see yourself truly letting go of the obstacles that you've chosen for a lifetime, you picture yourself no longer needing to rely on those self-defeating patterns. Then, the thinking part is complete. Now you move forward to a new you. When you leave behind the belief that you cannot change, or that you cannot create the miracle you want for yourself, you will leave behind the physical activity that has supported that belief. Picture it behind you, look back at it and know that you no longer live that way.

I can see myself at a distant time actually behaving in those old ways. And I smile inwardly, knowing that I have left that part of me behind. It started with a thought and then an action based on the new thought, and for me this is a miracle that I now live every day. I did it not by constantly trying to outthink the problem or by gradually sneaking up on it but by leaving it behind me. This is in fact the way all miraculous changes are made, when it gets right down to

"How do I change?" or "How do I create the miracle that I want my life to be?"

After all the talking, counseling, support groups, medicines, elixirs, pep talks and proddings by others, one must ultimately leave behind that which is self-destructive or functioning as an obstacle to growth. Every single person who has ever overcome any difficulty or brought about positive change in their lives, when faced with the bottom line, has had to leave behind the old habit through their own will. Know this to be a truth and you'll soon see yourself creating real magic in your life.

6. *When you examine what you believe to be impossible, you can then change your beliefs.* Take an inventory of what it is that you believe cannot happen in your life. Whether it is related to your physical accomplishments, relationships, health or finances, vow, at the very minimum, to rid yourself of these beliefs. I am not asking that you fool yourself or engage in self-deception. I am asking you to create an openness to the possibility rather than continuing to subscribe to the impossibility. That's all. Just an openness to a new idea. And remember, you do not have to do anything different in your life at this moment, only change around some mental images. New thoughts will ultimately lead you to new and miraculous behaviors.

If anyone has ever overcome a diagnosis of "terminal," then know that such a capacity exists within all of us. The universal force or energy that once created a miracle is still present. The force itself has not disappeared, even if the miracles themselves have. Stuart Wilde writes in *Miracles*, "Because the universal law is indestructible and therefore infinite, we can presume that whatever power was used by miracle workers in the past must still be available today." And if it is still available, I am asking you to believe that it is there for you to tap into. This universal law that created miracles has not been repealed, and never will be.

This entire book is about helping you align yourself in such a way that this universal force or energy is something that you can know intimately, and use in your life, even if no one else around you knows what you are doing or believes in what you are talking about when you speak of miracles. Once you know and choose to use this force, your life will take on the flavor of real magic. I guarantee it.

At this point I am not asking you to begin performing miracles. I am asking you to simply open yourself to a new inner belief system that says maybe, just maybe, this is a possibility for me. Everyone who has ever come from dirt-poor origins to create abundance for themselves (including myself) has had to use the universal energy within their minds before it could happen in the physical world. If that miracle-making power was available to any impoverished soul, it is available to your impoverished soul should you decide that this is your truth.

Know that if anyone has gone from sickness to health, fat to slim, addiction to choice, poor to rich, clumsy to agile, miserable to happy, or discontentment to fulfillment, then that capacity is part of the universal human condition. Even if only one person has ever accomplished it, then it is indeed possible. And, even if it has never been before—such as a cure for polio prior to 1954, or an airplane ride in 1745— the fact that one unique individual is capable of conceiving it in his or her mind is all that is required for humankind to be open to the possibility. Replace the belief that something you are capable of imagining in your mind is impossible with the belief that it is possible. Go to work on that thought right now, in this moment, which is the only physical reality you have.

7. *You can go beyond logic.* Although you may not be completely comfortable relying on something other than logic and rational thinking, try to let in the idea that there is another dimension that is very much a part of you, which has nothing to do with logic or scientific validation. You have never seen, touched, smelled or physically felt a thought or a dream or a feeling, yet you know they exist. There is no rational proof for the existence of intuition, yet you know that it exists within you. Until a few years ago there was no physical proof for the presence of microscopic life, yet it existed. And so it is with a portion of your humanity that I call your soul. While we haven't come up with a

"soulscope" to rationally prove its existence, we have, nevertheless, an inkling that such a dimension persists as part of our humanness. There are some who will never believe it unless they see it. Others will see it because they believe it.

These are the seven beliefs you can use as mental steps to setting your internal gyroscope for real magic. There are some who live their entire lives content with the limitations of their five senses. Real magic and miracle making are not on their life agenda. For others, like you and me, while we know the physical part of us to be a beautiful miracle in and of itself, we also know there is a spiritual dimension, beyond the scope and boundaries of our physical universe. The differences between these two awarenesses—physical only versus spiritual *and* physical—are many. The next chapter will describe in more detail what these specific differences are and how the benefits of real magic and miracle making become available by shifting your consciousness to include your spiritual side.

THE TEMPLETON PLAN

From one of Wall Street's wisest investors comes a tried and true guide to personal growth and well-being. By following John Templeton's 21-step program — one step a day for three weeks — vital, connnections between beliefs in religious principles and belief in yourself are revealed, enabling you to become a successful and happy person.

IF ONLY HE KNEW

Gary Smalley explains a woman's deepest needs, shows a man how to meet those needs, and gives ten simple steps to strengthen any marriage. He helps men to understand not only how to respond to a woman's feelings, but also how to make her feel important. This invaluable guide filled with case histories and biblical examples maps a blueprint to a better marriage for today's modern man.

FOR BETTER OR FOR BEST

What motivates men and what natural qualities do women use to build a better marriage? In the tradition of Deborah Tannen's bestselling *You Just Don't Understand*, Gary Smalley helps women to understand not only the way men think, but also how to move a man's heart. With empathy, humor, and wisdom, Smalley solves every practical and emotional problem a woman can face in her marriage.